# MOZART'S JOURNEY TO PRAGUE

# EUROPEAN CLASSICS EDITIONS:

de ALARCON, R. A.
*The Three-cornered Hat*

von CHAMISSO, A.
*Peter Schlemihl*

von DROSTE-HÜLSHOFF, A.
*The Jew's Beech*

von EICHENDORFF, J.
*Memoirs of a Good for Nothing*

von GOETHE, J. W.
*Kindred by Choice*
*The Sufferings of Young Werther*

GOTTHELF, JEREMIAS
*The Black Spider*

HAUPTMANN, GERHART
*The Heretic of Soana*

HOFFMAN, E. T. A.
*The King's Bride*

MERIMEE, PROSPER
*A Slight Misunderstanding*

MÖRIKE, EDUARD
*Mozart's Journey to Prague*

de la MOTTE-FOUQUE, F. H. K.
*Undine*

STORM, THEODOR
*Viola Tricolor* and *Curator Carsten*

WALSER, ROBERT
*The Walk and Other Stories*

THREE GERMAN CLASSICS
*Immensee* by Theodor Storm, *A Village Romeo and Juliet* by G. Keller, *Lenz* by George Buchner

von GRIMMELSHAUSEN, J. J. C.
*Simplicius Simplicissimus*

HOFFMAN, E. T. A.
*The Devil's Elixirs*

KELLER, GOTTFRIED
*Green Henry*
*Martin Salander*

OVID
*The Art of Love*

ANTHOLOGY OF SPANISH LITERATURE

# MOZART'S JOURNEY
# TO PRAGUE

BY

## EDUARD MÖRIKE

TRANSLATED BY

## LEOPOLD VON LOEWENSTEIN-WERTHEIM

JOHN CALDER
LONDON

This translation from the German first published
1957 by John Calder (Publishers) Ltd.,
18 Brewer Street, London W1R 4AS.

Reprinted November 1964
Reprinted February 1976

ISBN 0 7145 0388 6 cased
0 7145 0389 4 paper

Printed by Unwin Brothers Limited,
The Gresham Press, Old Woking, Surrey.

# CONTENTS

# INTRODUCTION

EDUARD MÖRIKE was born on September 8th, 1804, at Ludwigsburg in Wuerttemberg. He was the third of seven children of Karl Friedrich Mörike, a distinguished doctor. He received his first education at the local Grammar School and after his father's premature death in 1818 entered the (Protestant) Seminary at Urach to prepare himself for the career which had been destined for him but for which he was temperamentally quite unsuited. In 1822 he took up the study of theology at Tuebingen where the most antiquated rigorous statutes still governed the studies and daily routine of theological students. He took little part in student life as such but cultivated a small circle of high-minded young men who shared his love for poetry and music. Very early on Mozart became his favourite composer. In Tuebingen he fell in love with a young Swiss girl, "Peregrina", an enigmatic figure who, disowned by her family for having joined an itinerant religious sect, captivated his imagination as much as his heart both on account of her great beauty and of the "saint-and-sinner" atmosphere which surrounded her.

Having passed his final examinations in 1826 he successively held a number of posts as vicar in rural parishes and was appointed parson (Pfarrer) of the parish of Cleversulzbach in 1834. During those years he frequently took leave of absence for reasons of health and devoted himself more and more to writing. His first collection of lyrical poems appeared in 1838, an autobiographical novel, *Maler Nolten* having appeared some years previously. In 1843 he retired on a small pension to live at Bad Mergentheim, but returned again to a more active life in 1851 when he was appointed teacher of German literature at the Katharinenstift at Stuttgart, an appointment he held until 1866. In 1851 he married Margarethe von Speeth by whom he had two daughters. The marriage was not a very happy one and in 1871 husband and wife separated to be re-united only shortly before Mörike's death. In later life many honours were bestowed on Mörike who, even during his lifetime, came to be regarded as one of Germany's foremost lyrical poets. Many of his poems were set to music by Hugo Wolf and other composers. Mörike died in Stuttgart on June 4th, 1875.

# CHRONOLOGY

1804 8th September born at Ludwigsburg, Wuerttemberg.

1811 Enters Ludwigsburg Grammar School.

1818 Death of father. Mörike moves to Stuttgart.

1818–1822 At the Seminary at Urach.

1822–1826 Studies Theology at the University of Tuebingen.

1826–1834 Various appointments as vicar to country parsons. Beginning of literary work (lyrical poems, etc.). First engagement (1829), broken off in 1833.

1832 *Maler Nolten* (Autobiographical novel).

1834–1843 Parson (Pfarrer) at Cleversulzbach.

1838 First edition of poems.

1843 Retires on a pension. Bad Mergentheim.

1846 *Idylle vom Bodensee.*

1850–51 *Mozart's Journey to Prague* (first published 1855).

1851 Appointed teacher of German literature at the Katharinenstift, Stuttgart.

1851 Marries Margarethe von Speeth.

1852 Honorary degree of doctor of philosophy of Tuebingen University.

1853 Prose fairy-tale: *Stuttgarter Huzelmaennlein.*

1855 Birth of first daughter.

1856 Made a professor.

1857 Birth of second daughter.

1866 Final retirement.

1871 Separates from his wife.

1875 4th June, dies at Stuttgart.

IN the autumn of the year 1787 Mozart, accompanied by his wife, travelled to Prague, there to produce his opera, *Don Giovanni*.

On September 14th, around eleven o'clock in the morning—it was the third day of their journey—the couple were not more than thirty hours travelling distance from Vienna, driving in high spirits to the northwest. They had left behind them Mount Mannhard and the German Thaya and were now close to Schrems, almost at the top of the beautiful Moravian mountain range.

"The conveyance, drawn by three post horses," wrote Baroness von T—— to a woman friend, "is a handsome orange-coloured coach, the property of an old lady, wife of a certain General Volkstett, who prides herself on her acquaintance with the Mozarts and the services she has been able to render them." Anyone familiar with the taste prevalent in the seventeen-eighties can complete this vague description of the vehicle with a few touches of his own. The doors on either side of the orange-coloured coach are adorned with bunches of flowers, painted in their natural colours, and wheels are decorated with a narrow, gold moulding. The paintwork, however, still lacks the mirror-like lacquer finish so characteristic of

13

present day Viennese coachbuilding, nor is the body fully rounded, though it tapers elegantly down to a bold curve. The roof is high and the windows are hung with stiff leather curtains, which at the moment are drawn back.

Here we might also say a few words about the appearance of the travellers themselves. The smart new clothes for official occasions had been carefully packed in the trunk and a simple travelling outfit chosen by Madame Constance for her husband. Over an embroidered waistcoat of a somewhat faded blue he wore his usual brown topcoat adorned with a row of large buttons, so fashioned that a layer of red-gold pinchbeck showed through the covering material, loosely woven in a starlike design. Black silk breeches, stockings and shoes with gilt buckles completed his costume. For the last half hour he has dispensed with his coat because of the unaccustomed heat and now sits there, talking animatedly, bareheaded and in his shirt sleeves. Madame Mozart is wearing a comfortable travelling dress striped in bright green and white. Tied in a loose bow, her beautiful, light brown hair falls abundantly over her neck and shoulders. Her curls had never been disfigured with powder while her husband's hair, plaited into a thick queue, was a good deal less powdered to-day than usual.

They had followed at a leisurely pace a road that led gently up between the fertile fields which here and there broke the extensive woodlands, and had now reached the edge of the forest.

"What a lot of woods we have passed," said Mozart, "to-day, yesterday and the day before. I hardly paid

14

any attention to them and it never even occurred to me that we might set a foot inside them. How would it be, dear heart, if we got out here? We might pick some of those bluebells growing so prettily over there in the shade. Hi! fellow," he called to the postillion, "you can give your horses a rest."

As the two rose a small mishap came to light, which cost the Maestro some scolding. Through his carelessness, a phial of very precious scent had come uncorked and its contents spilled over his clothes and the cushions of the seat.

"Oh, dear, I thought that was what had happened," complained Madame Mozart, "I've been noticing a strong smell for quite a little time. There's a whole bottle of real *Rosée d'Aurore* gone in a minute and I've been saving it like gold."

"Never mind, little one," he tried to comfort her. "Don't you see that in this way the heavenly perfume has been of real use to us? There we were, sitting in this oven of a coach and all your fanning brought us no relief. Then all of a sudden the whole carriage was cooler and you thought it was due to a few drops of scent I had put on my ruffles. We were quite revived and our conversation continued happily when just beforehand our heads were drooping like those of sheep on the way to market. So we shall reap the benefit of this little accident for all the rest of our journey. Now let us put our Viennese noses into the green wilderness."

Arm in arm they crossed the ditch at the side of the road and plunged into the shade of the fir-trees, which became denser and deeper, until only an occasional

15

sunbeam pierced the darkness to light up the velvety moss underfoot. The delicious coolness, in stark contrast to the blazing heat outside, could have been risky for the carefree fellow had it not been for the loving foresight of his companion, who with some difficulty managed to persuade him to put on his coat, which she had held in readiness.

"Heavens! What a glorious sight!" he exclaimed, looking up at the stately trees. "One might be in a church. I feel as if I'd never been in a forest before nor realized what it meant—a whole tribe of trees standing together! No hand of man has planted them. They have sprung up of themselves and there they stand, simply for the joy of living and growing side by side. Do you know, when I was young I used to travel backwards and forwards across half Europe; I saw the Alps and the sea, the grandest and most beautiful sights in the world. But now, simpleton that I am, I stand in an ordinary firwood on the frontiers of Bohemia, astonished and entranced that such things exist, and not, as it were, only as *una finzione di poeti*, like nymphs and fauns, and the like nor even as a forest on a stage, but growing out of the soil, reared up by moisture and the warm light of the sun. This is the abode of the stag, carrying his fantastic antlers on his brow; of the quaint squirrel, the mountain cock and the jay."

He stooped down and broke off a toadstool, praising its magnificent vermilion and the delicate white gills on its underside, and also put into his pocket an assortment of fir cones.

"One would think," said his wife, "that you never

ventured twenty paces in the *Prater*, where you could
find all these rarities."

"The *Prater!* I like that—how can you compare
them? Why, with the carriages, swords of state, finery,
fans, music—with all the show of the great world,
what else can you possibly see? Why the very trees, no
matter how important they try to look—I don't know
what it is—but the nuts and acorns on the ground
are hardly distinguishable from the hosts of broken
corks mixed up with them. From two hours off the
wood smells of waiters and sauces."

"Fancy that!" she exclaimed, "from a man who
enjoys nothing so much as eating fried chicken in the
*Prater*."

Back in the coach once more the pair resumed their
journey. The road continued level for a little while
before it gradually began to slope downhill through a
smiling landscape which lost itself at last in distant
hills.

"Truly the earth is beautiful," resumed the Maestro
after a long silence, "and we can blame no one for
wanting to remain on it as long as possible. Thanks
be to God, I feel as young and well as ever and am in
the mood to do a thousand things, which will have
their turn as soon as my new work is finished and produced. How many remarkable and beautiful things
there are—wonders of nature, or science, of the arts
and crafts—in the world, both near and far, of which
I know nothing yet. I am sure there are many things
about which I know as little as the blackfaced lad
sitting by his charcoal kiln over there; but yet there
has always been in me a burning desire to look into

17

this, that and the other, which is not my immediate stock-in-trade."

"The other day," she replied, "I came upon your old pocket calendar for the year 1785. You had jotted down several memoranda on the back. The first one says that in the middle of October the great lions are being cast at the Imperial brass foundry. The second, underlined twice, reads: Visit to Professor Gattner. Now, who is he?"

"Quite right, I remember. It's the dear old gentleman at the Observatory who keeps on inviting me. For a long time I have wanted to take you with me to look at the moon and the man in it. They have a mighty great telescope there now and I'm told that one can see the vast disc through it, brightly and clearly as if you could touch it, with mountains, valleys and ravines and, on the side on which the sun does not shine, the huge shadows thrown by the mountains. For the last two years I've been meaning to go there but I haven't got round to it yet, I'm ashamed to say."

"Well, well," she replied, "The moon will not run away. We shall catch up with things in time."

After a short silence he continued :

"Isn't it the same with everything? It hardly bears thinking of, what one misses, postpones or leaves undone—without even mentioning our duty towards God and man—simply in the way of enjoyment and of those little, innocent pleasures, which are spread out before us every day."

Madame Mozart could not, or did not try to, deflect him from the line of thought which his emotional nature was now following and unfortunately had to agree with him wholeheartedly as he continued with mounting emphasis.

"Have I ever enjoyed the company of my children even for as much as an hour?" he demanded. "How half-hearted and rushed I always am about that kind of thing. I take the boys on my knee once in a while or romp around the room with them for a couple of minutes and then Basta! off with them again. I can hardly remember that we spent a happy day together in the country at Easter or Whitsun, in a garden, wood or meadow—just ourselves, playing with flowers, having fun with the children, so as to become a child again oneself. And all the while, faster and faster, life goes by. Good God, if one stops to think, how terrifying it really is!"

These self-reproaches had unexpectedly given their intimate and affectionate conversation a serious turn. We shall not relate it in detail but rather take a look at the conditions, which now provided the immediate and express topic of their discussion, now merely formed the background to what they said.

Here we must above all admit to the sad fact that this passionate man, who was so responsive to the allurements of the world and yet could reach out to the loftiest spiritual heights—much as he had experienced, enjoyed and created in the short span of his life—had always lacked the happy conviction of achievement. The ultimate cause of this discontent may well lie no deeper than in those inherent, apparently insuperable weaknesses of character which we, not without reason, are inclined to regard as the

19

inevitable complement to the very qualities we most admire in Mozart. His needs were many-sided and, above all, his taste for the pleasures of social life was exceptionally strong. Sought after and acknowledged by the most distinguished families of the city as an incomparable genius, he rarely, if ever, refused an invitation to a party, a soirée or a ball. Besides this, he also liked to entertain his own, more intimate friends. For instance, on Sundays he would never forego the customary musical evening at his house, nor would he do without those informal luncheon parties, two or three times a week, when he gathered his friends and acquaintances round his well-appointed board. Sometimes, to the dismay of his wife, he would bring guests to the house—without notice as it were, straight from the street—people of widely varying merit, dilettanti, artists, singers and poets. The idler, whose sole virtue lay in his unfailing good humour and wit, however unsubtle, was as welcome as the gifted connoisseur or the accomplished musician. But on the whole, Mozart looked for his relaxation outside his own home. He would play billiards at the café every day after lunch, and many an evening he could be seen at the tavern. He liked to make up a party to drive or ride out to the country and, an accomplished dancer, frequently attended balls and masquerades. Once or twice a year he greatly enjoyed himself at public festivals, especially at the open-air fête during St. Bridget's Fair, where he would always appear in the costume of a pierrot.

These pleasures, now colourful and boisterous, now attuned to a more gentle mood, were necessary to give his mind a rest after the intense strain of prolonged intellectual effort. Besides, they conveyed to him, along those mysterious channels through which genius unconsciously operates, those fleeting impressions which stirred his inspiration to life. Unfortunately, however, at those times other considerations such as prudence, duty, self-preservation or domestic responsibilities, were of little account because his one concern was to drain the happy moment to its last drop. Both in his pleasures and his creative work, Mozart knew no bounds.

Part of the night was always given to composition, and in the morning, lying late abed, he would revise and elaborate on what he had written. Then, at about 10 o'clock, he would set out, either on foot or with a carriage to pick him up, to make his round of lessons, which generally occupied part of the afternoon as well.

"We are working extremely hard to make ends meet," he wrote once to a patron, "and at times it is difficult not to lose one's patience. One goes out as a competent pianoforte player and music teacher, saddling oneself with a dozen pupils and taking on yet more without regard to their talents, as long as they pay their thaler per lesson. They're all welcome—any mustachioed Hungarian officer in the Corps of Engineers, driven by the devil to study bass and counterpoint for no apparent reason or purpose whatsoever; any high-spirited little countess, who receives me scarlet with anger, as though I were Master Cockerel the hairdresser, if for once I don't knock on her door exactly on the stroke of the clock. . . ."

21

When tired out by these and other professional labours—classes, rehearsals and the like—instead of the breathing space for which he longed, fresh excitements would, more often than not, provide the only stimulus for his jaded nerves. All this steadily undermined his health which, in turn, if it did not actually cause, at least contributed to the periodic attacks of depression which tormented him. Thus his premonitions of an early death which, in later years, dogged his every step, were inevitably fulfilled. Sorrow of every kind and description, including the sense of remorse, had given a tang of bitterness to his life. Yet we know that all these sorrows converged purified in the deep source of his genius, to spring serene in the inexhaustible golden fountain of his melodies, wherein all the tribulations and happiness of the human heart are expressed.

It was in Mozart's home that the ill-effects of his way of life showed themselves most plainly. The reproach of foolish and improvident extravagance was often justified and unfortunately must be applied to some of the noblest instincts of his heart. If anyone in urgent need approached him for a loan or backing, it was a foregone conclusion that Mozart would not ask for a pledge or inquire into the security given. He was as incapable as a child of making such a request. He preferred to give a present outright and always with a kind of laughing magnanimity, especially when he believed himself at the moment to have something to spare.

The means to meet such expenditure, apart from the normal needs of the household, would have been out of all proportion to his actual income. The revenues derived from theatres, concerts, publishers and pupils, together with the pension from the Emperor, were all the more inadequate because the taste of the public was still far from having declared itself definitely in favour of Mozart's music. Its pure beauty, richness and depth bewildered his listeners after the popular and easily digested fare to which they were used. It is true that, thanks to the popular elements in the work, the Viennese public could not, at the time, have too much of *Belmonte and Constance*;[1] but a few years later *Figaro* unexpectedly proved a sorry failure —at any rate in comparison with the enchanting but infinitely less important *Cosa Rara*[2]—and this was not due entirely to the intrigues of the management; the same *Figaro* which immediately afterwards the sophisticated—or perhaps unprejudiced—citizens of Prague received with such enthusiasm that the Maestro, touched and gratified, decided to write his next great opera for Prague.

Despite the unpropitiousness of the age and the influence of his enemies, Mozart might have been able, with a little circumspection and prudence, to derive considerable material benefit from his art. But as it was, he was usually the loser even with those ventures in which the great public gave him their enthusiastic approval. In short, everything seemed to conspire—fate, character and his own mistakes—to prevent this unique man from prospering.

We can easily understand how difficult the position

[1] Die Entführung aus dem Serail.
[2] Light opera by Martìn y Soler (Trans. Note).

of a conscientious housewife must have been under these conditions. Although very young and happy-go-lucky and, as the daughter of a musician, something of a Bohemian herself as well as accustomed to privations in her own home, Constance made strenuous efforts to stop the rot at its source, to curtail some of her husband's excesses and to offset by small economies the large-scale waste. It was in this latter that she may have lacked the right touch and proper experience. She kept the money and the household accounts; every bill, every demand from their creditors, every-thing unpleasant or untoward, went exclusively to her. Thus at times she was driven almost to despair, especially when her husband's melancholia was added to their want and distress, their painful embarrassment and fear of open disgrace. For days on end he would sit idle and inaccessible to consolation, dwelling end-lessly, either with sighs and laments to his wife, or silent and absorbed all by himself in a corner of the room, on the sad idea of death. However, her courage rarely failed and as a rule her quick intelligence found a way out of their difficulties, if only for a time. But on the whole she could not improve matters much. If, for instance, she succeeded one day, by serious plead-ing or flattery, to cajole him into having tea with her or dining at home with the family and not going out again, what had she really gained? Overcome at see-ing tears in her eyes, he might sincerely foreswear some bad habit and promise even more than she had asked; but in vain—he would soon be back on his old course. One is almost tempted to think he could not do other-wise; and that a totally different way of life, in accordance with our conception of what is right and proper for most people, would, if forced upon him, have destroyed this unique personality.

Nevertheless, Constance continued to hope for a favourable change insofar as this could come from outside : by a radical improvement of their economic position which, with the growing fame of her husband, could not be forever delayed. If only, she thought, the pressure of anxiety which he, now more, now less, constantly experienced, could cease; if, instead of devoting half his time and energy to making money he could live and follow his true vocation undividedly; if he could at last enjoy his pleasures with a clear conscience instead of chasing after them, such relaxation would benefit him in mind and body and his whole inner condition would become easier, calmer and more natural. She envisaged an eventual change of domicile, hoping that his exclusive preference for Vienna, where she was convinced he would never have any luck, might yet be overcome.

The next decisive step towards the realization of her hopes would come, Madame Mozart promised herself, from the success of the new opera, which was the object of their present journey.

The composition had now progressed well beyond the first half. Close friends, who were qualified to judge and who were familiar with the origin of this extraordinary work and thus had an adequate grasp of its character and range, spoke of it everywhere in such terms that even many of his enemies were prepared for this *Don Giovanni* to take the entire musical world by storm from one end of Germany to the other before half a year had gone by. Other well-wishers, more cautious and reserved, basing their views on the trend of contemporary music, did not dare to hope for a general and quick success. The Maestro himself, in his inmost heart, shared their only too well-founded misgivings.

As for Constance, as women do when guided by emotion and spurred by a most justifiable desire, she held fast to her belief, undeterred by those later misgivings which generally assail men. Just now in the carriage she had again had occasion to defend her point of view. She did so in her gay and engaging manner and with redoubled energy because, in the course of the previous conversation, which was doomed to lead nowhere and therefore ended inconclusively, Mozart's spirits had noticeably dropped. With the same gaiety, she now explained to her husband in great detail how she would use, on their return, the hundred ducats which he had received from the Prague producers for the score, to cover the most urgent debts as well as for other things; and also how she hoped to manage on her budget throughout the winter and into the spring.

"Your Mr. Bondini[1]," she said, "can be relied upon to feather his nest with your opera. But if he is half as honest a man as you always make him out to be, he will surely give you a tidy percentage of those sums which the various theatres pay him for the score; and if not, thank God, there are other possibilities in

[1] The manager of the Opera Company which produced *Don Giovanni* in Prague. (Trans. Note).

view and a thousand times more solid ones, too. I have all sorts of ideas about that."

"Out with them then."

"A little bird told me the other day that the King of Prussia was looking for a Kapellmeister."

"Oh?"

"Director General of Music, I mean. Let's dream about it a little. I have that weakness from my mother."

"Go on, the taller the tale the better!"

"Not at all. Let's just assume that in a year from now———"

"On the Greek Calends. . . ."

"Be quiet, Tom Fool. I say that a year from now, around St. Giles's day, there must be no trace of an Imperial Court composer answering to the name of Wolfgang Mozart to be found anywhere in Vienna."

"How you run on!"

"I can hear already what our old friends will be saying about us and all the stories they will tell."

"Such as?"

"For instance, one fine morning at about nine o'clock, our old admirer, Madame Volkstett is crossing the Kohlmarkt with the impetuous stride reserved for important visits. She has been away for three months. That famous journey to her brother-in-law in Saxony, which has been the subject of our daily conversation ever since we have known her, has at last come about. She got back last night and now, with a heart bursting with the joys of travel, with friendly impatience and all sorts of delightful gossip, she rushes to the Colonel's wife, up the stairs, knocking on the door, not waiting

27

for the 'Come in!'; just try to imagine the welcome, the embraces, the good ladies' joy. 'Now, my dear Mrs. Colonel,' says Madame Volkstett, after some preliminaries, 'I bring you a host of greetings—I wonder if you can guess from whom? I haven't come from Stendhal direct—we made a little detour to the left towards Brandenburg.' 'What?' cries the other, 'Do you mean to say you went to Berlin? Were you visiting the Mozart's?' 'Ten heavenly days!' 'O my dear, my sweet, my incomparable Mrs. General, tell me all about it. How are those dear little friends of ours? Do they like it there as much as at first? It's fantastic, I can still hardly imagine—less so than ever now that you've seen them—Mozart as a Berliner. How does he behave, what does he look like?' 'Oh, I wish you could see him!' exclaims Madame Volkstett, 'The King had sent him to Karlsbad this summer. Can you imagine his dearly-beloved Emperor Joseph doing that? They had both only just returned when I arrived. He is sparkling with life and health, plump and vivacious as Mercury, with happiness and contentment written all over his face.' "

And now Constance, in her assumed role, began to paint a picture of their imagined future in the brightest colours. From their apartment in Unter den Linden and their house and garden in the country, to the brilliant scenes of Mozart's public activities and the exclusive Court circles in which he had to accompany the Queen on the piano—so vivid was her description that it all appeared immediate and real. Whole conversations and charming anecdotes were conjured up like rabbits out of a hat. She really seemed to be more

familiar with the Prussian Court, with Potsdam and
Sans Souci, than with Schoenbrunn and the Imperial
Burg in Vienna. In her story, she was mischievous
enough to endow her hero with a number of entirely
new domestic virtues which had developed in the solid
soil of Prussia; among which Madame Volkstett
quoted as the most remarkable example of how far the
pendulum can swing, the beginnings of a sound streak
of avarice, which she had noticed and which was
infinitely becoming to him.

" 'Just think, he receives his salary of three thousand
thaler for what? Twice a week he conducts the Grand
opera and once a week he gives a chamber concert.
I saw him—our dear little treasure of a man, surrounded by his magnificent orchestra, which he has
trained and which adores him. I sat with Madame
Mozart in her box just across from the Royalties. And
what was on the bill, do you think? I've brought one
along for you—and here's a little present from me
and the Mozart's wrapped up in it. Just take a look,
read it, there it is printed in letters as large as life——'
'Heavens above! Not *Tarar*?' 'Two years ago, when
Mozart wrote *Don Giovanni* and that confounded
spiteful sneak, Salieri,[1] was already secretly scheming
how he might on his own territory repeat the success
he had carried off in Paris with his own piece; and he
and his henchmen were already plotting how they
might cunningly set about to put *Don Giovanni* on
the stage in a nicely plucked condition, neither dead

[1] The Italian composer, now only remembered because of his
intrigues against Mozart at the Imperial Court and Opera in
Vienna. (Trans. Note).

nor alive, as they had done with *Figaro*. . . . Well, at that time I made a vow never to see that abominable piece for anything in the world. I kept my word, too. Everybody rushed to the play, including you, dear Mrs. Colonel. But I stayed by my own stove, my cat on my lap, and ate my bit of tripe. I did the same on the following occasions. And now, would you believe it? *Tarar* at the Berlin opera. Mozart himself conducting the work of his arch-enemy. You must sit through it, Mozart called out to me after the first quarter of an hour, if only so that you can tell them in Vienna that I have not allowed a hair of Absalom's head to be touched. I wish he were here himself, the dog-in-the-manger, to see there's no need for me to make a hash of someone else's work in order to maintain my own position.' "

"Brava, Bravissima !" cried Mozart at the top of his voice, and taking his little wife by the ears, he began to kiss and cuddle her. And so this delightful game—blowing coloured soap-bubbles and dreaming of a future which unfortunately never came to anything even in the most modest way—ended gaily in laughter and caresses.

Meanwhile for some time they had been dropping into the valley and were now approaching a village which they had seen from the height and behind which, in the friendly plain, there stood a small castle in the fashionable style, the seat of a Count von Schinzburg. In this village they had decided to stop for lunch and to feed the horses. The inn where they pulled up stood by itself at the end of the village, on a road from which branched an avenue of poplars, some six hundred paces long, leading to the grounds of the castle.

When they had alighted from the carriage, Mozart as usual left the ordering of the lunch to his wife. Meanwhile he demanded for himself a glass of wine to be brought into the parlour; Madame Mozart asked only for a glass of fresh water and some quiet corner where she might rest for an hour or so. She was shown upstairs, her husband following after, singing and whistling to himself. In a whitewashed room which had been hurriedly aired for them there stood, among other pieces of fine old furniture—which had no doubt found their way here from the castle—a clean and elegant bed with a painted canopy supported on green lacquer posts. The original silk curtains had long been replaced by ones of a more ordinary material. Constance prepared to settle down on the bed. He promised to wake her in time. She locked the door after him and he went down to look for entertainment in the general parlour. But not a soul was there except the inn-keeper and since the conversation of the latter was as little to his taste as the wine, he expressed a desire to go for a walk in the direction of the castle before lunch. He was told that the park was open to respectable visitors and that the family happened to be away for the day.

He had soon covered the short distance to the open park gates and then proceeded slowly along an avenue of ancient lime trees, from the end of which he suddenly saw the front of the castle, a little to his left. It was built in the Italian style, the walls washed in a light colour and a double flight of stone steps leading to the door; the slate roof was decorated with a few statues in the fashionable manner—gods and goddesses —and surrounded by a balustrade. He walked between large flower beds still in profuse bloom, and made his way towards the wooded part of the park. He passed some fine groups of dark Italian pines and gradually returned along winding paths towards the more open parts of the garden. Attracted by the vivid splash of water, he presently came upon a fountain. Around its wide oval pool orange trees in tubs stood in an ordered array, interspersed with oleander and laurels. The whole was girdled by a soft, sanded path, off which opened a narrow trellised arbour; it seemed a most pleasant place to rest. A small table stood in front of a bench and here Mozart settled himself.

Idly lending his ear to the music of the fountain, and letting his eyes rest on an orange tree of medium height and laden with golden fruit, which stood quite close to him outside the circle round the pool, our friend was led from the contemplation of this scene of southern beauty to delightful memories of his own youth. With an absent smile, he reached for the nearest fruit, savouring its exquisite rounded shape and juicy coolness in the hollow of his hand. Entwined with the scene from childhood which this had evoked, a long-forgotten musical memory rose before him and for a while his mind dreamily followed its uncertain trail. And presently he looks about him with sparkling eyes; he is captured by an idea which he immediately pursues. Immersed in his thoughts, he again touches the orange, which this time comes off the branch into his hand. He is so far away in his artistic remoteness that he sees but does not notice what he has done and, humming to himself almost inaudibly the beginning or middle of a melody, he twirls the scented fruit under his nose. Instinctively he brings out of his side pocket an enamelled box from which he takes a small knife with a silver handle and slowly begins to sever the golden globe from top to bottom. He may perhaps have been guided by some feeling of thirst, yet he was content simply to breathe in the fruit's delicious scent. For minutes on end he gazed at the two inner surfaces; then put the halves together again, only to open them and join them to each other once more.

Suddenly he hears footsteps close by. He gives a start and the consciousness of where he is and what he has done dawns upon him. He makes a move to hide the orange but stops himself, either out of pride or because it is already too late. The head gardener, a tall, broad-shouldered man in livery is standing before him. He had, no doubt, seen Mozart's furtive gesture and was at a loss for what to say. Mozart, equally speechless and riveted to his seat, looked at the gardener half laughing but blushing visibly. Then, with a challenge in his blue eyes—for an onlooker this must have been extremely funny to watch—he put the apparently undamaged orange in the centre of the table with a kind of defiant emphasis.

"I beg your pardon," the gardener began with ill-concealed annoyance, after taking a look at the not very distinguished outfit of the stranger, "I don't know whom I have——"

"Kapellmeister Mozart from Vienna."

"You are known at the castle, no doubt?"

"I'm a stranger here. I'm just stopping on my way to Prague. Is his Lordship at home?"

"No."

"And her Ladyship?"

"She's busy and won't see anyone."

Mozart got up and started to leave.

"Pardon me, sir," said the gardener, "how did you come to do such a thing in a place like this?"

"What the devil do you mean?" exclaimed Mozart, "Do you think I meant to steal and gobble up the thing?"

"Sir, I believe what I see. These oranges are counted and I am responsible. This tree has been ordered specially for a party by his Lordship. We are just about to take it away. I can't let you go until I have reported this incident and you yourself have given a satisfactory explanation."

"Very well," said Mozart, "I'll wait here. You may depend on that."

The gardener looked round with some hesitation and Mozart, thinking that all he wanted was a tip, put his hand in his pocket; but he had not a penny on him.

The two under-gardeners now appeared on the scene, put the tree on a barrow and carried it away.

Meanwhile the Maestro had taken a sheet of paper from his wallet and while the gardener stood over him, began to write in pencil:

"Most Gracious Lady,
Here I sit, a wretch in your paradise, like Adam

34

after he had eaten the apple. The damage has been
done and I cannot even blame Eve, who at this
very moment is innocently sleeping in a fourposter
at the inn, with Cupids and Graces hovering
around. Command me, your Ladyship, I am at
your disposal to answer for my extraordinary mis-
deed.

In sincere confusion, your Ladyship's humble
servant,

W. A. Mozart,
on his way to Prague."

He handed the note rather clumsily folded to the
uneasily waiting servant and told him to deliver it to
the Countess.

No sooner had the gardener disappeared than a
carriage could be heard entering the courtyard on the
other side of the castle. It was the Count, bringing
home a niece of his and her fiancé, a wealthy young
Baron from a neighbouring estate. The mother of the
latter had not gone out for many years and therefore
the engagement had been celebrated at the Baron's
home. Now there was to be another party with a
number of relatives here where Eugenie had, since her
childhood, been like another daughter to the Count and
Countess. The Countess had come home a little before
with her son Max, the lieutenant, in order to make a
few final arrangements. With their arrival the corri-
dors and staircase were thrown into a cheerful commotion so that the gardener had some difficulty in
catching the Countess in the ante-room and handing
her the note. However, she did not unfold it

immediately and without paying much attention to what the messenger said busily continued with her own affairs.

He waited and waited but she did not re-appear. Servants hurried by—footmen, ladies' maids, valets. He asked for the Count and was told he was changing. He looked for Count Max and found him in his room, deep in conversation with the Baron. But his story was cut short by the Count, as if he had been trying to report or ask for instructions on a subject which should still be kept secret.

"Go away. I'll be with you in a minute," said his young Lordship.

He hung about for a little while until at last father and son emerged at the same time from their rooms to hear about the calamity.

"Devil take him!" exclaimed the stout, goodhearted but choleric gentleman. "That goes beyond a joke! A Viennese musician, did you say? Some sort of a vagabond, no doubt, trying to beg his way and meanwhile taking what he can find."

"I beg your pardon, your Lordship. He doesn't look quite that sort. I don't think he's quite right in his head. He's very haughty, too. His name seems to be Moser. He's waiting in the garden for your answer. I told Franz to keep an eye on him."

"And what's the good of that now? Even if I shut the fellow up, the damage is done. I have told you a thousand times that the front gates should be kept shut. The mischief could have been prevented if you had carried out my orders."

At this moment the Countess hurried in from the

next room, waving an open letter with joyful excitement.

"Who do you think is in the garden?" she cried, "Read this, for heaven's sake! Mozart—you know, the composer from Vienna. We must ask him in at once. I'm only afraid he may have gone. What will he think of me? And you, Velten," she said, addressing the gardener, "were you polite to him and what really did happen?"

"What happened?" repeated her husband, whose anger was not immediately mollified by the prospect of a visit from such a famous man, "the damned fellow has picked one of the nine oranges on the tree we had chosen for Eugenie. The rascal! The whole point of our little pleasantry has gone and Max may as well scrap his poem."

"Oh, never mind!" pleaded the Countess, "the gap can easily be filled. Just leave it to me. And now go along, the two of you, release the good man and welcome him as politely and warmly as you can. He should, if you can manage to persuade him, break his journey here to-day. If you don't find him in the garden go to the inn and bring him along with his wife. A better present, a more beautiful surprise for Eugenie, could hardly have come our way."

"Indeed," replied Max, "that's how I feel, too. And now hurry up, Papa, come with me. Don't worry," he added, as they made their way hastily towards the staircase, "about those verses of mine. The Ninth Muse will not be neglected. On the contrary, I shall turn this mishap to good account."

"Impossible!" snorted his father.

"Not at all. I'm sure we can."

"Well, if you think so—I'll take you at your word —we'll have to show that unruly fellow all the courtesy we can."

While all this was going on at the castle, our prisoner, unconcerned with the outcome of the matter, passed his time in writing. But after a while, when nobody seemed to appear, he became a little restless and began to pace up and down impatiently. In addition, an urgent message had come from the inn that lunch was waiting and would he come immediately because the postillion was anxious to get moving again.

He gathered up his things and was about to leave when the two gentlemen appeared outside the arbour. Loud-voiced and animated, the Count greeted him almost like an old friend. He gave him no time to make any apologies but immediately expressed his wish that the couple should stay at least for luncheon and spend the evening with his family.

"My dear Maestro," continued the Count, "you are no stranger—indeed, I may say that there's hardly a place where the name of Mozart is mentioned more often and with greater enthusiasm than here. My niece sings and plays. She spends practically the whole day at the piano. She knows your works by heart and I know she is longing to see you more closely than was possible at your concert last winter. We were thinking of going to Vienna shortly for a few weeks and she has been promised an invitation to Prince Galitzin, where you can often be met. But now you are going to Prague, you probably won't be back so soon and

God knows whether your return journey will bring you this way again. Make a break to-day and to-morrow. We can send the carriage back and perhaps you'll allow me to take care of the rest of your journey."

The composer, who on such occasions was always prepared, for the sake of friendship or pleasure, to sacrifice ten times more than was asked of him in this particular instance, did not hesitate for long. He agreed joyfully to stop for the rest of the day but said that early next morning they must continue on their way. Count Max asked for the pleasure of fetching Madame Mozart and making all the necessary arrangements at the inn. He went off on foot and a carriage was to follow him immediately.

We should mention in passing that this young man combined with a friendly disposition inherited from his father and mother, a talent and love for the fine arts, and though he had no real calling to a military career, distinguished himself as an officer by his wide knowledge and strong sense of duty. He was well acquainted with French literature, and at a time when society had little regard for German poetry, the not inelegant form of his own verses in his mother tongue, modelled on good examples in the works of Götz and Hagedorn, had won favour and praise. To-day he had, as we have already mentioned, a specially joyful occasion to make use of his talent.

He found Madame Mozart chatting with the inn-keeper's daughter. She was already sitting at the table and was about to start on a plate of soup. Accustomed as she was to unexpected developments and to her

husband's whims, the sudden appearance and mission
of the young officer did not surprise her unduly. Calm
and sensible, and with obvious pleasure, she immediately made all the necessary arrangements. Trunks
were repacked, the bill was paid, the postillion dis-
charged and then, without undue haste, she got herself
ready and in high spirits was driven with Count Max
to the castle, not suspecting in what strange fashion
her husband had introduced himself there. The latter,
meanwhile, had installed himself very comfortably and
was being looked after in the best possible way. He
had already met Eugenie, a lovely girl in the flower
of her youth, and her fiancé. She was fair and slender,
wearing a dress of lustrous crimson silk trimmed with
costly lace and around her brow was a white fillet,
adorned with pearls. The Baron, only a little older
than she, seemed to have a gentle and open disposition
and to be worthy of her in every way.

At first the good-humoured master of the house did
most of the talking, interspersing his conversation
almost too liberally with jokes and humorous anecdotes. Refreshments were served, to which our traveller
helped himself freely.

The score of *The Marriage of Figaro* lay open on
the piano and the young lady was about to sing,
accompanied by the Baron, Susanna's aria in that
famous garden scene in which the stream of sweet
passion breathes like the spiced air of a summer night.
The delicate pink on Eugenie's cheeks gave way for
a moment to extreme pallor but when the first notes
burst from her lips her shyness vanished. Smiling
and self-possessed, she was poised on the high crest of

40

the wave and her sense of the uniqueness of this moment—for the whole of her life perhaps—seemed to transfigure her.

Mozart was obviously greatly surprised. When she had finished, he walked up to her and said in his warm and unaffected manner :

"What can one say, my dear child? It would be like praising the sun, whose best praise is that everyone feeling its glow is happy. Such singing makes the soul feel like a child in its bath: it laughs and wonders and can think of nothing more delightful in the world. Besides, believe me, it is not every day, even in Vienna, that the likes of us can hear ourselves interpreted with such purity and warmth, indeed with such complete perfection."

With these words he took her hand and kissed it cordially. Mozart's amiability and kindness, not less than the homage which he paid her talents, moved Eugenie so deeply that her eyes filled with tears.

At this moment Madame Mozart arrived and immediately afterwards other guests who were expected : a Baron and his family, close relations and neighbours, whose daughter Francesca had since childhood been an intimate friend of Eugenie.

There were greetings, embraces and congratulations all round. The two Viennese guests were introduced and then Mozart sat down to the piano. He played part of a concerto which Eugenie had been studying for quite some time.

The effect of such a recital in a small circle of this kind naturally differs from that of a recital in a public

41

place by the far greater satisfaction which immediate contact with the artist and his genius affords within one's own four walls. It was one of those brilliant pieces in which pure beauty, as if by a whim, places itself freely at the disposal of elegance; yet in such a way that it is only thinly disguised, as it were, in these wanton and playful forms and, hidden behind a mass of brilliant fireworks, betrays in every movement its own innate nobility, exuberantly pouring forth its own magnificent ardour.

The Countess could not help remarking to herself that, notwithstanding the solemn silence that greeted this enchanting recital, the attention of most of the listeners, Eugenie not excepted, was divided between ear and eye. Looking at the composer as he sat there, unassuming and almost awkward in his attitude, with his kindly face and the rounded movements of his small hands, it was difficult to resist a flood of speculations at this miraculous little man.

When the Maestro had finished, the Count turned to Madame Mozart.

"When it comes to bestowing informed praise on a distinguished artist," he said, "not everybody has the aptitude for it. How I do envy kings and emperors at such times! The fact is that in their mouths almost anything sounds remarkable. There's nothing they can't get away with. For instance, how delightful to stand just behind the chair of your husband and, after the last chord of a brilliant fantasy, to slap the modest classical gentleman on the shoulder and say: You are a devil of a fellow, my dear Mozart! No sooner out, the words spread like wildfire through the room. What did he say? He called him a devil of a fellow. And the whole bunch of fiddlers, composers and music lovers are beside themselves over this expression; in short, the fine, homely Imperial style, that inimitable style of the Josephs and the Fredericks, which I have always envied and never more so than now when I am completely at a loss for some apt and fitting words of praise."

Such waggish remarks from the Count were always engaging and as usual produced a storm of laughter.

Presently the Countess invited the whole party to repair to the small, circular dining-room where, after the heat of the *salon*, a cool breeze and the scent of flowers lent a delicious edge to their appetite. They took their seats in fitting order—the distinguished guest opposite the engaged couple. On one side he had a small elderly lady, an unmarried aunt of Francesca and on the other, the charming young niece herself, whose intelligence and vivacity aroused his interest at once. Madame Constance sat between the master of the house and her charming escort, the lieutenant, and the others disposed themselves as they liked. They were a party of eleven, sitting informally round the table, of which the lower end was left empty. On it stood two huge pieces of Dresden porcelain —painted figures holding wide bowls heaped with fruit and flowers. The walls were hung with rich draperies.

The whole setting and everything that followed seemed to promise a full-blown feast. On the table between the plates and dishes and on the sideboard in the background, were many noble wines, from deepest crimson to the pale gold whose sparkling bubbles form the traditional crown of such a banquet.

Up to now, the conversation, sustained in the liveliest manner on all sides, had turned on general subjects. But as the Count who had, right at the beginning, dropped some veiled hints about Mozart's garden adventure, now began to allude to it more directly, so that some of the party smiled slyly to themselves while others tried in vain to guess what he was talking about, our friend felt bound to come out with the whole story.

"In God's name," he began, "let me confess how it came about that I have the honour to have made the acquaintance of this noble house. My role was not very dignified. I had a narrow escape and, instead of dining and wining here, I might have been sitting in the remotest corner of the castle prison looking with an empty stomach at the cobwebs on the wall."

"Well!" exclaimed Madame Mozart, "Now we shall hear a pretty tale."

He now described in detail how he had left his wife at the White Horse Inn, his walk in the park, the mishap in the arbour and his encounter with the custodians of order in the garden; in short, he told everything we already know, with complete candour and to the infinite delight of his listeners. It seemed as if the laughter which greeted this story would never end and even the restrained Eugenie was shaken with mirth.

"Well," said Mozart, "the proverb tells us that he

44

who has the profit can face the laughter and I've certainly had my profit out of this. You'll see presently. But listen now how it really happened that an old fool could so forget himself. A memory of my youth had something to do with it. In the spring of 1770, when I was a lad of thirteen, I travelled with my father to Italy. We went from Rome to Naples. I had played twice at the Conservatoire and given other private recitals. The nobility and dignitaries of the Church showed us great courtesy, in particular one *abbate*, who had quite some influence at Court and considered himself something of a connoisseur. The day before our departure he, together with some other gentlemen, took us to the royal gardens—the Villa Reale—stretching along a magnificent road by the seashore, where a troupe of Sicilian comedians were giving a performance. *Figli di Nettuno* they called themselves, among other high-sounding names. We were part of a noble audience, which even included the charming young Queen Caroline and two princesses, sitting on a long row of benches in the shade of a low loggia covered with a tent-like canopy. The sea splashed against the wall of the terrace beneath our feet. In ribbons of many shaded blue, the water reflected the brilliance of the sky. Facing us was Mount Vesuvius and the gently curving coastline shimmered on our left. The first part of the entertainment was over. It was given on a raft, anchored off the shore, and there was nothing very remarkable about it. The second and more beautiful part, however, consisted of a series of water tableaux—swimming, diving and nautical displays. The whole thing, in every detail, has remained

45

fresh in my memory. Two elegant, lightly-built vessels, both as it were on a pleasure trip, approached each other from opposite sides. The larger of the two had a half-deck and rowing benches and a slender mast with a sail. It was beautifully painted with a gilded prow. Five youths, of magnificent physique, their arms, legs and chests naked, were either rowing or disporting themselves with the same number of ravishing maidens—their sweethearts. One of them, more beautiful than the rest, who was sitting in the centre of the deck, weaving garlands of flowers, far outshone the others in figure, face and attire. They served her willingly, fixing an awning to protect her from the sun and handing her flowers from a basket. A girl sat at her feet playing a flute, which accompanied the singing of the rest. This exquisite creature also had her beau but the pair seemed rather indifferent to each other; indeed, the attitude of the lover appeared to be one of disdain.

"Meanwhile, the smaller, plainer vessel had approached. Here one saw only young men clad—by contrast with the crimson worn by the youths in the first ship—in garments of green. They looked startled at the sight of the lovely maidens and, greeting them with waves and signs, tried to convey their desire to know them better. Thereupon, the gayest of the girls plucked a rose from her bosom and playfully held it aloft, as if to ask whether such a gift might be acceptable. This gesture produced an unmistakable response from the other boat. Sombre and contemptuous, the red youths looked on, but there was little they could do when some of the girls started to try to assuage the

46

hunger and thirst of the poor devils in green. A basket of oranges—no doubt only yellow balls painted to look like the fruit—stood on the deck. And now began a delightful performance, accompanied by the playing of an orchestra gathered on the edge of the water. With a graceful movement, one of the maidens tossed a few oranges across to the other boat. They were as gracefully caught and immediately returned. Thus the golden fruit flew to and fro and, as more and more girls joined in, oranges were soon whizzing across by the dozen at ever-mounting speed. The beautiful girl in the centre of the red boat took no part in this but watched the contest eagerly from her little stool. One could not praise too highly the adroitness shown by both sides. The ships, about thirty paces apart, slowly circled each other. Now they lay broadside on, now their prows seemed almost face to face. About twenty-four balls must have been constantly in the air, though in the general confusion one thought one could see many more. At times they kept up a regular cross fire. Then again the missiles rose and fell in a wide curve. Hardly any missed their mark. It looked as if of their own accord, or the mere power of attraction, they fell into the open palms.

"While the eye was thus pleasantly regaled, the ear feasted on a selection of enchanting airs—Sicilian folksongs, dances, saltarelli, canzone a ballo—loosely strung together like flowers in a wreath. The younger of the two princesses, a lovely unaffected child of about my own age, gently nodded her head in time with the music. I can see to this day her long eyelashes and the way she smiled.

47

"And now I must just tell you how the performance went on though it has no bearing on my own story. You could hardly imagine anything more charming. As the skirmish gradually subsided into a few single shots and the girls began to collect their golden fruit and return them to the basket, a boy in one of the boats playfully took up a wide green net and let it down into the water. He pulled it in and, to everyone's astonishment, there shimmered a large blue-green and gold fish. His companions sprang forward eagerly to help disentangle the fish from the net but it slipped through their hands as if it really were alive and fell back into the sea. This was, of course, a stratagem to fool the reds and lure them out of their ship. The latter, as if bewitched by this wonder and seeing that the fish, instead of diving kept playing on the surface of the waves, did not hesitate long but with one accord jumped into the sea. The greens immediately did likewise and there one saw twelve well-developed and powerful swimmers in pursuit of the fleeing fish, which now seemed to leap from crest to crest and now dived into the depths, to re-appear between the legs of one or the chest and chin of another of the swimmers.

"Suddenly, while the reds were in hot pursuit of the prey, the others saw their advantage and, quick as lightning, made for their opponents' ship and jumped down among the screaming girls. The noblest of the greens, tall and slim as a Mercury, flew with a beaming look towards the queen of the girls and drew her to him in a passionate embrace and, far from joining in the screams of the others, she flung her arms warmly

48

round his neck. The band of hoodwinked lovers in the water hastily swam to the rescue but were repulsed by the greens with oars and weapons. Their unavailing fury, the anguished shrieks of the girls, some of whom resisted fiercely while others contented themselves with cries for mercy : all as it were almost drowned by the general commotion, the splashing of the water and the music, which had suddenly assumed an entirely different character—it was beautiful beyond description, so that the spectators broke into a storm of applause. At this moment the sail, which had been loosely furled, unfolded to reveal a rosy Cupid, with silver wings, bow, arrows and quiver, which hovered gracefully over the deck. Already the oars are busy and the sail swells to the wind, but more compelling than either seemed to be the presence of the god, waving the ship powerfully forward at such a speed that the breathless pursuers—one of whom held the golden fish aloft in his left arm—soon gave up exhausted and were forced to repair to the other, abandoned ship.

"By now, the greens had reached a small, bushy peninsula from behind which a stately ship, bristling with arms, unexpectedly made its appearance. In face of such threatening developments, the little band of greens ran up a white flag as a sign that they wished to parley. Encouraged by a counter-signal, they made for the anchorage and soon one saw the girls, with the exception of their queen who remained behind voluntarily with her captor, happily reunited with their lovers from the other ship. With this the pageant ended."

49

"I feel," whispered Eugenie with shining eyes, while everyone expressed their approval of what they had just heard, "that we have seen a whole symphony in colour, a perfect example of the spirit of Mozart in its gayest guise. Don't we see the whole charm and gracefulness of *Figaro* in this?"

Her fiancé was about to convey this remark to Mozart when the latter continued:

"Seventeen years have now gone by since I last saw Italy," he said, "but who, having once seen it, especially Naples, would not think of it for the rest of his life—even if he had been no more than a child as I was. But never before has the memory of that beautiful evening in the Gulf of Naples returned to me so vividly as to-day in your garden. When I shut my eyes—brilliant, distinct and clear, without the thinnest veil to obscure it—the divine landscape lay before me: the sea, the coast, the mountains, the city, the colourful crowds lining the shore and then that strange fantastic ball game over the water. I thought the same music was in my ear—a whole gay garland of melodies, my own and other people's, danced through my head. Then as if from nowhere, a little dance tune sprang up in my mind—something entirely new in six-eight time. Halt! I said to myself, what's this? A devilish enchanting air! I looked more closely—Heavens, if that isn't Masetto and that Zerlina!" He turned laughingly to Madame Mozart, who at once guessed his meaning.

"The point is simply this," he continued, "in the first act a small, lighthearted number remained unfinished—a duet and chorus for a rustic wedding. Two

50

months ago, when I attempted to tackle it in its proper order, it did not quite come off. A tune, simple and childish, sparkling with gaiety—that's what it had to be—like a posy of fresh flowers with fluttering ribbons, pinned to a girl's dress. Since one should never try to force things and such trifles have a way of solving themselves, I simply passed it over and, pressing on with the main part of the work, hardly gave it another thought. Fleetingly in the carriage this morning, as we approached the village, I thought of the words of the song; and that, as far as I knew, was all. But an hour later, in the arbour beside the fountain, I captured a motif—a happier and better I cannot imagine finding at any other time or place. Sometimes in art strange things happen to one but nothing like this has ever happened to me. The melody seemed to fit the words like a glove—but I'm rushing ahead, I hadn't got there so fast. The little chick was only just peeping out of the egg and so I set to work to set it free completely. Meanwhile Zerlina's dance was vividly before my eyes, mingling in a strange way with the laughing landscape of the Gulf of Naples and I heard the voices of the bridal pair answering each other against the chorus of the maidens and youths."

And now Mozart began to hum the opening bars of the gay little song :

"Giovinette, che fatte all'amore, che fatte all'amore,
Non lasciate, che passi l'età, che passi l'età, che passi
   l'età !
Se nei seno vi bulica il core, vi bulica il core,

51

Il remedio vedete lo quà! La la la! La la la!
Che piacer, che piacer che sarà!
　　　Ah la la! Ah la la, etc." [1]


"Meanwhile, my hands had done great damage and
Nemesis, which had been waiting round the corner,
now stood before me in the guise of this terrifying
man in his braided blue livery. A sudden outbreak of
Vesuvius on that divine evening by the seashore, covering and burying the spectators and actors and all the
glory of the Parthenope under a black rain of ashes—
why, such a catastrophe could not have been more
unexpected and alarming. The old devil! no one has
ever made me feel quite so uncomfortable. A face
as stern as if cast in bronze, resembling the cruel
Roman Emperor Tiberius. If that's how the servant
looks, I thought when he had left me, what will his
Lordship himself be like? But to tell you the truth,
I was already banking on the protection of the ladies
and not without good reason; for my little wife here,
who is inquisitive by nature, got our stout landlady
at the inn to tell her everything most worth knowing
about all the personages composing this illustrious
family; I happened to be standing by and so I
heard——"

[1] "Maidens who are made for loving,
Let not love's season pass you by.
If in your bosoms your hearts are yearning
Cupid to cure you is standing by.
　　La la la, La la la!
What pleasure, what joy yours will be!"
(Free translation from the original Italian). There is also an
English version of this in Boosey's edition of *Don Giovanni*.

At this point Madame Mozart could not help interrupting him to declare with emphasis that, on the contrary, he had been doing the questioning. Thus a gay argument started between husband and wife which gave rise to much merriment all round.

"Be that as it may," said Mozart, "In short, I heard something of a beloved foster-daughter, who was engaged to be married, very beautiful and kindness itself and singing like an angel. *Per Dio*, I thought, that will help me out of the mess. Sit down at once and write the little song, explain as best you can the peccadillo and hope it gives them a good laugh. No sooner said than done. There was just enough time and luckily I found a clean sheet of lined paper in my pocket. Here is the result. I confide it to these beautiful hands—an impromptu wedding song, if you will accept it as such."

He handed a neatly written sheet of music across the table to Eugenie, but her uncle's hand was quicker than hers. Snatching it away, he exclaimed:

"Patience, my child, wait just a little longer."

At a sign from him the double doors leading into the drawing room were flung open and some men-servants carried in that fateful orange tree and set it down, decorously and silently, on a bench at the lower end of the table. At the same time a slender myrtle tree was placed on each side of it. An inscription fixed to the trunk of the orange tree declared that it was the property of the bride. On the moss in front of it, however, there was a plate covered by a napkin. This latter was removed to show an orange cut in half beside which the uncle now cunningly put the

53

Maestro's autographed manuscript. Tumultuous applause greeted this.

"I almost believe," said the Countess, "that Eugenie has no idea yet what is standing before her. She does not seem to recognize her old favourite in its new guise and all decked out with fruit."

Startled and incredulous, the young girl looked now at her uncle, now at the tree.

"It's impossible," she said at last, "I knew quite well it couldn't be saved."

"Do you mean to say," answered the uncle, "that we have chosen a substitute? That would have been a shabby thing to do! Just take a look. I shall have to proceed after the manner of the comedies, where sons or brothers reported dead have to prove their identity by a birthmark or a scar. Look at this protuberance and here, the crack in the trunk. If you've seen them once, you've seen them a hundred times. Now is it the same tree or isn't it?"

She could doubt no longer and she was surprised, delighted and touched beyond words.

A hundred-year-old memory was linked for the family with this tree—the memory of a remarkable woman who well deserves that we should mention her here. The Count's grandfather, outstanding in the Imperial Cabinet through his great diplomatic gifts and honoured by the confidence of two successive sovereigns, enjoyed the added blessing of a most excellent wife, Renate Leonore. Her frequent visits to France brought her into contact with the brilliant court of Louis XIV and with some of the most eminent men and women of that remarkable age.

Though joining without constraint in the perpetual whirl of highspirited pleasure, she never fell short in any way, by word or deed, of her innate German sense of honour and moral rectitude. These traits were unmistakably printed in the face of her portrait which hung on the wall. Owing to this mentality, she played the role in that society of an original and objective critic and her correspondence shows many traces of how, with great frankness and ready wit, this outstanding woman defended her wholesome principles and outlook in matters of religion, literature, politics or anything else and how well she could attack the weaknesses of that system without ever making a nuisance of herself. Such was her integrity, that her lively interest in the kind of people who used to meet in the house of Ninon de Lenclos—the true centre of refined cultural and intellectual life—did not clash with her exalted friendship with Madame de Sevigny, one of the noblest women of her age. As well as some gay epigrams by Chapelle, written in the poet's own hand on sheets of paper bordered with silver flowers, a number of loving letters from the Marquise and her daughter to their good friend from Austria were found in a small ebony casket after the Countess's death.

It was from the hand of Madame de Sevigny that she received one day, on the terrace of the garden during a fête at the Trianon, a flowering orange twig which, almost without thought, she planted in a pot and, since it struck root, later took back with her to Germany. For some twenty-five years, the little tree grew up under her eyes and was later tended with the greatest care by her children and grandchildren. Apart from its personal value, it was to the family a symbol of the allure and sophistication of an age which they almost idolized; in which, however, we see to-day nothing truly laudable and which carried within itself a calamitous future, whose world-shattering onset was not far distant at the time of our innocent little tale.

It was Eugenie who lavished the greatest devotion on the legacy of their remarkable ancestress and for this reason her uncle had often remarked that one day the tree should belong to her. It was, therefore, all the more grievous to the young lady when, in the spring of the previous year which she had not spent at the castle, the tree began to show signs of wilting, its leaves turning yellow and many branches dying off. Finding that there were no special reasons for this decline and that nothing he did was of any avail, the gardener soon gave the tree up for lost, though in the natural order of things, it should have lived to twice or three times its age. The Count, on the other hand, acting on the advice of an expert in the neighbourhood, had the tree secretly treated in accordance with some strange—indeed mysterious—lore, such as country folk often possess. His hope of one day surprising his beloved niece with the sight of her old friend restored to new vigour and fertility succeeded beyond all expectation. Overcoming his impatience and not without anxiety that the fruit, some of which was already fully ripe, might fall off the branches, he had postponed the pleasure of this surprise for several weeks, until to-day's celebration. It is not difficult to imagine the feelings of the good gentleman when, at the very last moment, he saw his pleasure's perfection blemished by a stranger's wanton hand.

The Lieutenant had found time before lunch to alter his poetical contribution to the solemn act of presentation and adapted his somewhat too serious verses by changing the end to fit the new circumstances. He now produced a sheet of paper and, rising from his chair, turned to his cousin and read out his verses, whose contents were briefly these :

A descendant of the famous tree of the Hesperides, which according to ancient tradition had grown on a western isle in the garden of Juno as a wedding present to her from Mother Earth and which was guarded by three tuneful nymphs, had desired for himself a like destiny, since the custom of presenting a glorious bride with a tree had long since been passed on to mortals by the gods.

After waiting in vain for many a long year, he at last has found a maiden who perhaps will fulfil his hopes. She seems to favour him and often seeks him out. But the laurel, crown of the Muses, standing proudly beside him at the edge of the fountain, has awakened his jealousy by threatening to turn the heart and mind of this talented beauty away from the love of men. In vain the myrtle tries to comfort him and to teach him patience by its own example. Finally, the continued absence of his beloved makes him pine away and, after a short illness, brings him to the point of death.

Summer brings her home from afar with a changed and happy heart. The village, the castle, the garden receive her with a thousand joys. More radiant than

57

ever, the roses and lilies look up to her, enchanted
and modest. The bushes and trees wave her welcome
but alas! for one of them, the noblest, she arrives too
late. She finds his crown withered and her fingers feel
his lifeless trunk and his branches' rattling tips. He
cannot see or recognize his mistress. How she weeps,
how freely the tender lamentations break from her
lips. From far away, Apollo hears his daughter's voice.
He comes and, stepping towards her, looks with com-
passion on her sorrow. At once, with his all-healing
hands, he touches the tree. A tremor runs through it;
now the dried-up sap swells powerfully under the
bark, now young leaves break forth and white blos-
soms open in ambrosian plenty over the boughs. And
now—is there anything that the gods cannot do?—
beautiful round fruits begin to form, three times three
—nine—to match the number of the Muses. They
grow and grow, shedding their childish green for an
ever-deepening golden hue. Phoebus—that is how
the poem ended:

> Phoebus overtells the pieces,
> Taking infinite delight.
> Yes, his mouth begins to water
> At this very moment even.
>
> With a smile, the god of music
> Plucks the ripest of the lot.
> Let us share the fruit, my lovely,
> Cupid also has his cut.

The poet received thunderous applause and was
willingly forgiven for the baroque twist in the last

stanzas, which seemed to belie the rest of the poem's moving tenderness. Francesca, whose natural good humour and wit had more than once responded to the sallies of Mozart or her host, now quickly left the room as if remembering something and soon returned with a dark English etching on a large frame, which had hung unnoticed under glass in a distant study.

"So it's true after all, what I've always been told," she exclaimed, as she stood the picture at the end of the table, "That there's nothing new under the sun. Now here we have a scene from the Golden Age and have we not lived it again to-day? I only hope that Apollo will recognize himself in this part."

"Bravo!" cried Max, "There he is, the handsome god, bending pensively over the sacred spring. And that isn't all—look over there, the old satyr behind the bush, spying on him. One could swear that Apollo is just thinking of some long-forgotten Arcadian dance-tune, taught him in his childhood by old Chiron to the accompaniment of a lute."

"That's just how it is!" Francesca agreed enthusiastically. She was standing behind Mozart and now continued, addressing him: "And have you noticed the fruit-laden bough drooping over the head of the god?"

"Quite right. It is the olive tree sacred to Apollo."

"Not at all. They are the most beautiful oranges and in a moment he will absentmindedly pluck one."

"No, rather," answered Mozart, "he will stop this teasing mouth with a thousand kisses." With these words, he caught her arm and swore he would not let

59

her go until she had offered him her lips; which she did in the end with little demur.

"Do explain to us, Max," said the Countess, "the meaning of the inscription under the picture."

"It is a passage from a famous ode of Horace, full of ardour and elegance. It has been magnificently translated. For instance, listen to these lines :

> "Here met the foe
> Fierce Vulcan, queenly Juno here,
> and he who ne'er shall quit his bow,
> Who laves in clear Castalian flood
> his locks, and loves the leafy growth
> Of Lycia next his native wood,
> The Delian and the Pataran both." [1]

"Beautiful, really beautiful," said the Count, "but here and there a little explanation is needed. For instance, 'he who ne'er shall quit his bow' simply means that he has always been a most diligent fiddler. . . . But what I was about to say : my dear Mozart, you are sowing discord between two tender hearts."

"I hope not. How?"

---

[1] This is Conington's translation of Horace III, IV :
> hinc avidus stetit
> Volcanus, hinc matrona Iuno et
> numquam umeris positurus arcum,
> qui rore puro Castaliae lavit
> crinis solutos, qui Lyciae tenet
> Delius et Patareus Apollo.

In the German text a translation by the poet Ramler of Berlin is mentioned.

"Eugenie envies her friend and she has every reason for it."

"Aha! You have spotted my weakness. But what is the bridegroom going to say?"

"Once or twice I will turn a blind eye," said the young man.

"Excellent! We shall take the opportunity. But you don't have to worry, my dear Baron. There is no danger as long as the god does not also lend me his features and his long golden hair. I wish he would! He could have in exchange Mozart's queue with its most handsome bow."

"But then Apollo will have to watch in future," said Francesca, laughing, "how to dip his latest French hair-do gracefully into the Castalian flood."

With these and similar pleasantries, the gaiety and spirits of the party mounted. The men were beginning to feel the effects of the wine. A great number of toasts had been drunk and Mozart, as was his habit, began to speak in verse. The Lieutenant entered into competition and Papa, not wishing to be outdone, joined in and succeeded once or twice beyond all expectation. But such trifles can hardly be retold. They do not lend themselves to repetition because what makes them irresistible in their right place— the heightened mood, the glitter, the direct impact of the speaker's words and expression—is lacking. Among other toasts, the elderly maiden aunt proposed one in honour of the Maestro, wishing him a long series of immortal works.

"A la bonheur! I'm all for it," exclaimed Mozart, clinking glasses heartily with her.

61

On this the Count began to sing, extemporising with great power and assurance.

> "May the gods give inspiration
> For the still unborn creation—

MAX *(continuing):*

> "Of which neither does Da Ponte,
> Nor that great man Schikaneder—

MOZART:

> "Nor, by God, the poor composer
> Know the slightest at the moment.

THE COUNT:

> "All of which we now are hoping
> That the rascally Italian—
> Signor Bonbonnière we call him—
> Lives to see to his discomfort.

MAX:

> "Good! A hundred years I give him,

MOZART:

> "Bar the devil in his wisdom—

ALL THREE *con forza*:

> "First has seized with all his ware
> Wicked Signor Bonbonnière!" [1]

The Count was so fond of singing that what had started, almost accidentally, as a trio soon developed, by the repetition of the last four lines, into a so-called *Canon finitus* and the maiden aunt had sufficient humour or self-assurance to add, in her quavering soprano, all sorts of grace notes and embellishments.

([1] This is how Mozart, when among friends, referred to his colleague Saliero who, wherever he was, nibbled at sweets and candies. It was an allusion also to the daintiness of his figure).

Afterwards, Mozart promised that, when he had more time, he would elaborate this little caprice for his friends, setting it out in accordance with the correct rules of composition : a promise which he did, in fact, carry out when he got back to Vienna.

Eugenie, meanwhile, had long since acquainted herself with the gem that had been composed in the arbor Tiberius, and there was now a general clamour that she and the composer should sing the duet. Her uncle was delighted at the chance to show off his voice once more in the chorus, so everyone rose from the table and made for the piano in the big *salon* next door. Pure as was the enchantment of this delightful piece, its subject soon led by a quick transition to the very heights of merrymaking, in which the music as such was of secondary importance; it was our friend who took the lead in this by jumping up from the piano, going towards Francesca and inviting her to a *Schleifer*[1] while Max eagerly picked up a violin. The host was quick to ask Madame Mozart to dance. In an instant, all the movable pieces of furniture had been shifted by bustling servants in order to make more room. Before the end everyone had to take the floor and the maiden aunt was only too pleased when the gallant Lieutenant led her out in a minuet in which she became quite young and skittish. Finally, when Mozart was dancing the last round with the future bride he redeemed in full his claim to her fair lips.

Evening was falling, the sun had begun to set, and now, at last, it was pleasant out of doors; so the Countess

[1] Slow gliding valse.

suggested to the ladies that they should go into the garden for a breath of air. The Count, however, invited the gentlemen to the billiard room, as Mozart was known to be extremely fond of the game. And so the company divided and we, for our part, will follow the ladies.

Having paced leisurely up and down the main avenue, they ascended a rounded hillock, half enclosed by a tall, vineclad trellis, from which one had a view of the open country, the village, and the main road. The last rays of the September sun, now setting, glowed red through the leaves of the vine.

"Wouldn't this be a quiet place to sit down for a little," said the Countess, "if Madame Mozart would care to tell us something of herself and her husband."

Constance declared herself willing and so they drew up the chairs in a circle and settled down comfortably.

"I'll tell you a story which you would have to hear in any case because a little joke which I am planning is connected with it. I have made up my mind to give the bride, as a happy memento of to-day, a present of a somewhat unusual kind. It is far from being an object of luxury or fashion; in fact, it is only by reason of its history that it is of some interest."

"What could it possibly be?" Eugenie asked Francesca, "It must at least be the inkpot of a famous man."

"You're not far wrong," said Constance, "and you'll see it this very hour. The treasure is packed in our trunk. I shall begin and, with your permission, I'll hark back a little way.

"The winter before last, increased irritability, frequent depressions and feverish excitement, had made us quite alarmed about the state of Mozart's health. When in company, he could be gay, sometimes almost unnaturally so, but at home he generally brooded by himself or grumbled and complained to me. The doctor ordered a diet, Pyrmont water and exercise away from the town. The patient paid very little heed to this advice; the cure was inconvenient, time-consuming and utterly opposed to his daily routine. But now the doctor tried to frighten him and he had to submit to a long lecture on the properties of the human blood—corpuscles, on breathing and inflammatory conditions,[1] things you never heard of; also about the nature of food and drink and how digestion was intended to work—all matters about which Mozart's ideas were as innocent as a five-year-old's. The lecture indeed made a deep impression. The doctor had not been gone half an hour when I found my husband in his room, pensively but with a brighter expression absorbed in the contemplation of a walking-stick, which he had brought to light from a cupboard full of old stuff and which I would not have thought he would even have remembered. It had belonged to my father—a beautiful cane with an imposing lapis lazuli top. No one had ever seen Mozart with a walking stick and it made me laugh. 'You see,' he exclaimed, 'I am about to throw myself wholeheartedly into the cure. I will drink the water, exercise every day out of doors, taking this

[1] Phlogiston is the word actually used, a term with which early chemists denoted the principle of inflammability. It was introduced by the German chemist, Georg Ernst Stahl, in 1702 and belief in the theory lasted for nearly a century.

staff with me. All sorts of ideas have occurred to me. It's not for nothing that others—I mean, gentlemen of mature age—cannot do without a walking stick. Our neighbour, the Councillor of Commerce—whenever he crosses the street to visit his crony his stick goes with him. Functionaries and professionals, chancellors and tradesmen, when they take their families for an outing on Sunday, all take their honest, well-worn canes with them. Above all, I have observed on the Stephanplatz,[1] a quarter of an hour before the sermon and the Mass, all the worthy burghers standing around in groups talking; and it is here that one can see how each of their quiet virtues—their diligence, orderliness, calm confidence and content—are as it were supported by those trusty sticks. In a word, there must be some special blessing and comfort on this patriarchal—if slightly vulgar—custom. Believe it or not, I can hardly wait until, with my good friend for company, I take my first constitutional across the bridge towards the Rennweg. We know each other a little already and I hope that our partnership has come to stay.'

"The partnership, however, was of short duration. After their third outing together, his companion did not return with him. Another was procured, which kept faith a little longer. Anyway, to Mozart's new hobby I ascribed a good deal of the perseverance with which, for three weeks, he obeyed the doctor's orders to some extent. We soon saw the results. He had hardly ever been so fresh, so cheerful and even-tempered. But unfortunately, he soon began to overdo

[1] The square in front of St. Stephen's Cathedral.

things and I had my daily argument with him over that. About this time it happened that, returning tired from the labours of a strenuous day, he went, in order to please a few curious visitors, rather late in the evening to a musical soirée—only for an hour, as he solemnly promised; yet these are just the occasions when, once he is seated at the grand piano and carried away by his playing, people take advantage of his good nature most. There he sits, like the little man in the Montgolfiere,[1] floating six miles above the earth, where he cannot hear the chimes of the clock. Twice that night I sent a servant; but in vain, he could not get to his master. At three o'clock in the morning, he came home at last. I made up my mind that I would be cross with him for the rest of the day."

At this point certain details were passed over in silence by Madame Mozart. The reader should know that at this particular soirée a certain young singer, Signora Malerbi, to whom Madame Mozart had taken exception with good cause, was likely to be present. This young woman from Rome had been employed at the Opera through Mozart's good offices; and there is no doubt that these favours from the Maestro were largely due to her coquettish wiles. According to some people, he had been under her spell for several months past and she had managed to keep him nicely on the rack. But whether this is true or greatly exaggerated, it is certain that she behaved later with impertinence and ingratitude towards him and even went so far as to make fun of her bene-

[1] Early balloon, called after its inventor, Montgolfier. It rose by means of heated air.

factor. She spoke completely in character when once, to a more fortunate admirer, she described him simply as "un piccolo grifo raso" (a little shaven pig's snout). That flash of wit, worthy of a Circe, was all the more wounding because, as one is bound to admit, it contained a grain of truth. On the way home from this party, at which, in fact, the singer had not made an appearance, one of his friends, under the convivial influence of wine and company, committed the indiscretion of telling him of these malicious sallies. He took it badly because it was, for him, the first completely unmistakable proof of his protégée's heartlessness. He was so angry that he did not even notice the chilly reception with which he met at his wife's bedside. Without pausing to draw breath, he told her about the slight, and this frankness leads one to suppose that his conscience was not so very guilty after all. He almost succeeded in arousing her pity, but she would not give in to this, not wishing to let him get off so lightly. When he woke from a heavy sleep, just before midday, he found that his little wife and the two boys had left the house and that the table was neatly laid for him alone.

There were few things that could make him so unhappy as when all was not pleasant, harmonious and gay between himself and his better half, and this would have been greater now if he had known what added worry she had been carrying about with her for the last few days—indeed, one of the worst which she, as usual wanted to keep from him as long as possible. Her ready money was all spent and there was no immediate prospect of any more coming in. Though he had no inkling of this domestic predicament, the heaviness of his heart somehow reflected the embarrassment and helplessness of their state. He had no desire to eat and could not stay at home. He finished dressing quickly in order to get away as soon as possible from the oppressive atmosphere of the house. On a piece of paper he left a note in Italian. "You've given me what I deserve. But please forgive me, I implore you, and be laughing again by the time I come back. I'm so wretched I could become a Carthusian or a Trappist—I'm almost in tears, I promise you." He picked up his hat but not his stick—that phase was behind him.

Having told the story on Madame Constance's behalf up to now, there is no reason why we should not continue to do so for a little. From his home, turning to the right, the dear man ambled pensively—it was a warm, somewhat overclouded summer afternoon—across what is known as the Hof and on, past the parish church of our Blessed Lady, in the direction of the Schottentor, where he ascended the Moelkerbasteil on the left, thus avoiding a number of his friends, who were just entering the city. Though undisturbed by the sentry, who was silently pacing up and down between the cannons he only stayed a few minutes to enjoy the beautiful view across the green slope of the glacis and the suburbs towards the Kahlenberg and, southwards, to the Styrian alps. The beautiful peace of nature was in strong contrast to his own inner state. With a sigh he resumed his walk, crossing the esplanade and then passing through the suburb known as the Alser-Vorstadt without a definite goal in his mind.

At the end of the Waehringer Gasse there was an inn with a skittle alley whose owner, a ropemaker, was well-known among the neighbours and country-folk whose road led them past the house, for the excellence of his wares and the quality of his cellar. There was the sound of bowling but with only a dozen customers about, nothing much was going on. An instinctive urge to forget himself among simple, un-assuming people made the musician stop. He sat down by a table, half shaded by trees, joining up with an inspector of wells from Vienna and two other worthy townsfolk. He ordered a small glass of wine and fell in with their idle talk, now and then rising to pace up and down or to watch the game in the skittle alley for a while. Close to the latter, at the side of the house, was the ropemaker's open shop—a small room stuffed with wares because, apart from the products of his own craft, all kinds of wooden utensils for kitchen, cellar and agriculture, as well as blubber, axle grease for wheels and an assortment of seeds, such as dill and carroway, were displayed for sale. A young girl, who waited on the customers and also had to look after the shop, happened to be busy at this moment with a peasant who, holding his little son by the hand, had just come in to make some purchases—a fruit measure, a brush and a whip. He would pick out something from the mass of objects, examine it, put it aside again; choose another and yet a third and then return, irresolute, to his first choice. There was no end to it. The girl left several times to wait on customers and returning, tried indefatigably, but with-out any pushing sales talk, to help him to come easily and pleasantly to a decision. With great pleasure, Mozart looked on and listened from the small bench near the skittle alley. Much as he enjoyed watching the kind and sensible behaviour of the girl and the calm and seriousness in her pleasant features, it was the peasant who interested him most and who, after he had gone away satisfied, gave the Maestro most to think about. He had completely put himself in the man's place, feeling with him the importance he had attached to this small transaction and how anxiously and conscientiously he had weighed up the different prices—only a matter of one or two pennies here and there. Then he thought of the man going home to his wife and telling her delightedly about his bargain; of the children waiting till he opened the knapsack which might contain something for them; of the wife, knowing he had saved his appetite till now, making haste to bring him a snack and a draught of his own apple cider.

If only, he mused, one could enjoy such happiness, dependent not on people but only on Nature and her bounty, however hardly it is earned. But in my art haven't I a special task ordained for me which, when it comes to the point, I would exchange with no one in the world? Yet doing it, why must I live in a way which is the very antithesis of such a simple and innocent existence? A small estate, if one had that, a little house near a village in a beautiful neighbourhood, and one would surely be a new man. The mornings spent diligently with my scores, all the rest of the time with the family; planting trees, overseeing my fields, in autumn the boys and I picking the apples and pears; from time to time a trip to town for a show or such like, and now and again a friend or two to stay in the house. What bliss! Well, one never knows, it may happen yet.

He went up to the front of the shop, spoke kindly to the girl and began to look more carefully at her wares. The close association between many of these and his idyllic day-dream made the clean, pale smoothness and even the smell of the wooden tools particularly attractive to him. It suddenly occurred to him that he might buy a number of things for his wife which would, in his opinion, please her and be useful. It was gardening tools that particularly caught his attention. A year or so ago Constance had, at his suggestion, rented a small allotment outside the Kaerntner Tor, where she grew vegetables; so, to begin with, a large new rake and a smaller one, together with a spade, seemed to him to answer the purpose. Weighing up further purchases, it does credit to his sense of economy that, after a short deliberation, he declined, albeit reluctantly, an extremely engaging butter-keg; while, on the other hand, a tall, wooden jug, adorned with a beautiful, carved handle, of no particular use, seemed to him an obvious choice. It was made of narrow strips of two different kinds of wood, light and dark alternately, tapering towards the top and well coated with pitch inside. Just right for the kitchen was a fine selection of cooking utensils—wooden spoons, rolling pins, chopping boards and plates of all sizes, as well as a container for salt of very simple design to hang on the wall.

Finally he looked at a stout stick, whose leather

covered handle was studded with round brass nails. As the strange customer even seemed to be tempted by this, the girl remarked with a smile that it was not really suitable for a gentleman.

"You're right, my child," he answered, "a butcher's apprentice on his journey would carry just such a stick. Away with it, I don't want it. As for the rest—everything else that I've chosen you'll deliver to my house to-day or to-morrow." With this he gave her his name and address. So saying, he returned to his table to finish his drink. Of his three companions, only the master tinsmith was still sitting there.

"It's a good day for the waitress," said the man, "her cousin allows her a penny in the florin on the sales she makes in the shop."

Mozart was now doubly pleased about his purchases and soon his interest in the girl was to become greater still.

"How are things with you, Krescence?" the tin-smith called out to her as she approached them, "and how is your locksmith? Will he not soon be working his own iron?"

"Goodness knows," she exclaimed, hurrying by, "I think that iron is still growing right back there in the mountains."

"She's a good girl," said the tinsmith. "She kept house for her stepfather for a long time and nursed him when he was ill. After his death it came out that he had got through all her money. So now she works for her kinsman here—she does absolutely everything —in the shop, in the tavern and for the children. She knows a decent fellow and they'd like to be

73

married—the sooner the better. But there's a hitch about it."

"What is it?" asked Mozart, "Has he no money also?"

"They've both saved something but it's not enough. A half share in a house with a workshop is just coming up for sale. It would be quite easy for the ropemaker to advance her the balance of what is needed to buy it but as you can imagine, he doesn't want to let the girl go so easily. He has good friends in the municipality and the guilds and so he can put all sorts of difficulties in the young fellow's way."

"Damn it!" cried Mozart so that the other was quite startled, and looked round to see if anyone were listening, "Is there no one who could see that justice is done and put these gentlemen in their place—the rascals! Just you wait—we shall catch them yet."

The tinsmith was on tenterhooks. He tried clumsily to tone down what he had said, almost eating his own words.

"You ought to be ashamed of yourself," Mozart interrupted, "the way you're talking now. That's how all you scamps behave when it comes to standing up for something." On this, he turned his back on the coward without further ceremony. To the girl, whose hands were full with new arrivals, he whispered as she passed. "Come early to-morrow morning and give my regards to your sweetheart. I hope all will go well with you both."

She was taken aback and had neither the time nor the words to thank him.

More quickly than usual, because the incident had

roused his blood, he retraced his steps to the glacis on top of which he then proceeded more slowly, making a detour in a wide semi-circle skirting the walls. Completely absorbed in the troubles of the poor lovers, he went through in his mind a list of friends and patrons who, in one way or another, might be able to help in the matter. However, as it was necessary to have a more detailed account from the girl before he could decide on any course of action, he thought it best to wait for this; and now his whole mind and heart flew ahead of his footsteps and was already at home with his wife.

He was inwardly certain of a friendly, even joyful welcome and kisses and hugs as he entered the door. Longing quickened his footsteps as he passed through the Kaerntner Tor. A little further on, the postman called out to him and handed him a small, but rather weighty package, on which he immediately recognized the clear and honoured handwriting. He goes into the next shop with the postman in order to sign for the package. Then, back in the street, he cannot wait to reach his house before tearing the seal open; half walking, half standing, he devours the letter.

"I was sitting by my workbox," Madame Mozart continued her story to the ladies, "when I heard my husband coming up the stairs and asking the servant if I were in. His voice and step sounded more gay and lively than I'd expected or than indeed pleased me at that moment. He went to his room but immediately came in to me. 'Good evening!' he said; I answered him meekly without looking up. After pacing up and down the room a time or two in silence, with a forced yawn he took the fly swatter from the back of the door—a thing which had never occurred to him before. 'How these flies do get in here!' he muttered to himself, and started to hit about him with all his might. This was something he had never allowed me to do in his presence because he could not bear the sound of it. Hmmm, I thought, when one does it oneself, especially if one's the man, it's somehow different. Besides, I hadn't noticed that there were so many flies as all that. His strange behaviour began to irritate me. 'Six at a blow,' he called out suddenly, 'Do you want to see?' No reply. Thereupon he put something on my pin-cushion, where I could not help seeing it, though I would not lift my eyes from my work. It was nothing more alarming than a little pile of gold, as many ducats as one might hold between the finger and thumb. He continued his antics behind my back, hitting out every now and then and talking to himself: 'That odious, useless, shameless breed—what is it in the world for, really?—Slap—Evidently only to be killed. Slap. And that I may say I can do pretty well. Nature study teaches us about the astounding rate at which these creatures propagate—Flip, flap, flip. But we know how to get rid of them in this house. Ah, maledette! disperate! Here's twenty more. Do you want them?' He came up to me and did as before. If I had hitherto been able to suppress my merriment, it was now no longer possible and I burst out laughing. He fell on my neck and we were soon both dissolved in giggles.

" 'But who is sending you this money?' I asked, as he poured the rest of the gold pieces out of the packet.

'From Prince Esterhazy, through Haydn. Just read the letter.' I read :

'Eisenstadt, etc.

'Dearest friend,

'His Serene Highness, my most gracious master, has charged me, to my very great pleasure, to send you the sixty ducats enclosed herewith. We have played your quartets again and His Serene Highness was, if possible, even more delighted and enamoured with them than the first time he heard them about three months ago. The Prince remarked to me (I must quote this verbatim) : When Mozart dedicated this work to you he thought he was honouring you alone; but I don't think he can mind if I see in it a compliment to myself as well. Tell him that I shall soon think as highly of his genius as you do yourself and more than that he can hardly expect. Amen, I added. Are you now content?

'Postcript : A word in the ear of your dear wife. Please kindly see to it that he says thank you without delay. It would be better to do it in person. We must make the most of this fair wind.'

" 'Oh, the angelic man—the heavenly soul!' Mozart exclaimed again and again; and it was difficult to tell which pleased him most—the letter, or the Prince's approval, or the money itself. Truth to tell, as far as I was concerned, it was the last which meant most to me at the time. We spent a happy evening together celebrating the event.

"Of the affair in the suburb I learned nothing,

either that day or in the days that followed. A whole week went by and no Krescence appeared; and my husband, immersed in a whirl of business, soon forgot the incident. One Saturday evening we had a few guests—Captain Wesselt, Count Hardegg and one or two others were making music. During an interval I was called outside and there was a pretty kettle of fish! I went back into the room and asked my husband: 'Did you give an order in the Alser-Vorstadt for a whole collection of wooden goods?' 'Goodness gracious!' he exclaimed, 'Is the girl outside? Do let her come in.' So in she came, friendly and beaming, carrying the rake and spade and with a full basket on her arm. She apologized for not having come sooner but she had forgotten the name of the street and only managed to find it to-day. Mozart took the things from her one by one and, very pleased with himself, handed them on to me. I accepted them all gratefully, with comments of pleasure and praise; but I was somewhat puzzled to what purpose he had bought the garden tools.

" 'But, of course, they're for your allotment by the banks of the Wien.' [1]

" 'Good Lord! We gave that up long ago because the water did so much damage and nothing ever grew. I told you at the time and you didn't object.'

" 'Really? And does that mean the asparagus we had last spring——'

" 'It always came from the market.'

" 'Why, if only I'd known!' he said, 'And there

[1] A small river, side arm of the Danube, then outside the city walls, now canalised.

78

I was praising them to you from sheer politeness be-cause I was really sorry for you and your gardening. They were miserable little things, no thicker than a quill.'

"The gentlemen were greatly amused and I at once had to give them some of the unwanted tools as a keepsake.

"Mozart now began to question the girl, encourag-ing her to speak quite freely. He promised that any-thing that could be done for her sweetheart should be managed discreetly, properly and without anybody being accused. She answered with such modesty, caution and delicacy that she won all our hearts and was finally dismissed with every possible assurance.

" 'Those people must be helped,' said the Captain, 'The tricks of the Guild are the least of it. I know someone who can fix that in no time. What really matters is to raise a little money towards buying the house, and the cost of furnishing, equipping it, and such like. How would it be if we announced a benefit concert in the Trattner Hall, leaving the entrance fee to the generosity of our patrons?'

"The suggestion was warmly received. One of the gentlemen picked up the salt cellar and said : 'As an introduction, someone should give a nice historical account of all this—describing Mr. Mozart's pur-chases and his philanthropic intentions. This magnifi-cent vessel will be placed on the table as a collecting box, with the two rakes to the right and left and crossed behind it by way of decoration.

"This actually did not happen, but the concert took place and raised a tidy sum. Other contributions followed so that the happy pair even had some over, while all other obstacles were quickly overcome. The Duscheks in Prague, our intimate friends, who are now going to put us up, heard the story and she, a genial and delightful woman, was intrigued by the idea of having some of the stuff. I therefore put aside what I thought would be most suitable for her and have it with me. But since we have unexpectedly found a new and dear fellow artist who, moreover, is about to set up her own home and would therefore not refuse an ordinary piece of household equipment which Mozart has chosen, I will divide my present; and so you have the choice between a handsome open-work chocolate whisk and the famous salt container, which the artist has tastefully adorned with a tulip. I would definitely recommend this latter piece; the noble salt is, as far as I know, a symbol of domesticity and hospitality, to which we want to add all our good wishes."

So much for Madame Mozart's story and it is easy to imagine with what merriment the ladies heard it and how gratefully they accepted the present. The rejoicings began afresh when, shortly afterwards, the objects were displayed in the presence of the gentlemen and this example of patriarchal simplicity was formally handed over; the uncle declaring that in the silver chest of its new owner and her most distant descendants it would hold as high a place as that famous work of art of the Florentine master in the collection at Ambras.[1]

[1] The reference is to Benvenuto Cellini's famous salt-cellar, formerly in the collection at Schloss Ambras in the Tyrol and now in the Vienna Kunsthistorische Museum. (Translator's Note.)

It was now nearly eight o'clock and tea was served. Soon, however, our musician was reminded of the promise he had made at luncheon to acquaint the party with his *Don Giovanni*, which was still locked up in the trunk but fortunately fairly near the top. He agreed without hesitation. It did not take long to explain the plot of the opera. And so the libretto was opened and the candles stood ready lit on the pianoforte.

If only we could evoke for our readers at least something of that extraordinary sensation with which sometimes even one isolated chord drifting through an open window (a chord which could only have come from there) can electrify a passer-by and hold him spellbound; could make him experience something of that delicious anguish with which in the theatre we face the curtain while the orchestra is tuning up. Is it not so? If on the threshold of any great and tragic work of art, be it *Macbeth, Œdipus* or what you will, there hovers an intimation of eternal beauty—was this not one of those moments when we should experience it most powerfully? Man at once longs and fears to be taken out of his ordinary self. He feels that the infinite will touch him; it constricts his heart while expanding his spirit, which irresistibly it draws to itself. Add to this the awe before a consummate work of art. The thought of enjoying a divine miracle, of being allowed to receive it as something which is part of us, carries in itself a quality of emotion—indeed a kind of pride —perhaps the happiest and purest which we are able to feel.

The party at the castle, however, was placed very

differently from ourselves. This work, which we have known all our lives, they were to hear for the first time. Apart from the good fortune of hearing it performed by its author, they were not nearly as well placed as we are to-day; because a pure and perfect interpretation was really not possible then and for one reason and another could hardly have been hoped for even if the whole had been given in its full and un-abridged form. Of the eighteen completed numbers, the composer most probably played less than half (in the account on which our story is based, we only find the last piece in this series, the Sextet, explicitly mentioned). It appears that he gave a very free rendering, for piano only, singing certain passages when he came to them and as it seemed appropriate; only two arias are mentioned as having been sung by his wife. As her voice is supposed to have been very powerful and lovely, we should like to think that one was Donna Anna's first aria: "You know now for certain the name of the traitor," and the other, one of Zerlina's two arias. Strictly speaking, so far as intelligence, understanding and taste were concerned, Eugenie and her fiancé, but particularly the former, were the only members of the audience whose appreciation was at all discriminating or worthy of the Maestro's art. They sat in the shadows at the far end of the room, the young girl motionless as a pillar and so transported by the music that, during the short intervals when the others expressed their approval by subdued applause or involuntary murmurs of admiration, she could hardly respond to the remarks which her fiancé addressed to her.

When Mozart had ended with the rapturously beautiful Sextet and, little by little, the flow of conversation reasserted itself, certain remarks made by the Baron seemed particularly to interest and please him. The talk dwelt on the end of the opera and on its première, which was provisionally fixed for the beginning of November. When somebody expressed the view that certain parts of the finale still represented a gigantic task, the Maestro gave a cryptic smile. Turning to the Countess, Constance remarked in a voice which he could not fail to hear :

"He still has something up his sleeve, which he is keeping a secret, even from me."

"You speak out of turn, darling," he said, "in bringing up this point. Only suppose I took it into my head to start afresh? And in fact I'm itching to do so."

"Leporello!" cried the Count, jumping up gaily and calling one of the servants, "Wine! Three bottles of Sillery."

"No, really," exclaimed Constance, "We shouldn't have any more. My dear young man still has his last glass to finish."

"And good health may it bring him!" cried the Count, "and the same for us all."

"Good Lord, what are we doing?" lamented Constance, looking at the clock. "It's nearly eleven and we have to start early in the morning. However shall we get off?"

"You shan't, dearest lady. It just can't be done."

"Things happen in a very strange way sometimes,"

began Mozart, "I wonder what my Stanzerl[1] will say when I tell her that the very piece of music she is now about to hear was born at exactly this hour of night and also on the eve of a journey."

"Really? When? It could only have been three weeks ago when you were just off to Eisenstadt."

"Quite right. And this is how it happened. I came home from dinner at the Richter's after ten o'clock, when you were already asleep and, as I'd promised, I wanted to go to bed early so as to get off in good time next morning. Meanwhile, Veit had, as usual, lit the candles on my desk. I mechanically put on my dressing-gown and it occurred to me to have a quick look at my last piece of work. But, O misery! Confounded and ill-timed officiousness of women! You had tidied up and already packed the score which I had to take with me; for the Prince had demanded a rehearsal of the *opus*. I searched, I grumbled, I cursed —all in vain. At this my eye fell on a sealed envelope from the Abbate—to judge from the ghastly scrawl in which the address was written. Yes—Yes, indeed— and in it he sent me the rest of his revised text, which I had not expected to receive for another month. I sit down at once and eagerly begin to read it and am enchanted at how well the fellow has understood what I had in mind. Everything was much simpler, more concise, and yet more powerful than before. The grave-yard scene, as well as the finale down to the hero's damnation, had been greatly improved in every respect. (You shouldn't, I thought, most admirable poet, have conjured up heaven and hell for the second

[1] Diminutive for Constance.

84

time for me without reaping your reward.) Now, as a rule it is not my custom to anticipate anything in composition, however tempting it may be. It is a bad habit for which one often has to pay. But there are exceptions; and the scene by the equestrian statue of the Commendatore and the threat from the grave of the murdered man which, all of a sudden, terrifyingly interrupts the night revellers, had already gripped my imagination. I struck a chord and felt that I was knocking on the right door, behind which lay in wait a whole legion of terrors to be let loose in the finale. Thus first an adagio emerged : D minor—only four bars; followed by a second phrase of five—this, I flatter myself, will produce an astounding effect on the stage, where the most powerful wind instruments accompany the voice. Meanwhile, listen to it—the best we can make of it on the piano."

Without more ado he put out the candles in the two candelabra standing beside him and that terrifying air : "Di rider finirai pria dell'aurora" rang through the deathly stillness of the room. From far away starry spheres the silver trumpet notes seem to fall through the blue night, to pierce the soul with the icy tremor of doom. "Chi va là? Who goes there? Answer!" one hears Don Giovanni ask. Then the voice rings out afresh, monotonous as before, bidding the impious youth to leave the dead in peace.

When the last echo of the ringing notes had faded away, Mozart continued :

"Now, of course, there was no stopping me. Once the ice breaks by the shore of a lake, the whole surface cracks and the sound is carried to the furthest edge.

Instinctively I took up the same thread further on at the supper party, when Donna Elvira has just left and the ghost, at Don Giovanni's invitation appears. Listen."

Now followed the whole, long, terrifying dialogue in which even the most matter-of-fact listener is carried to the limits of human imagination and beyond; where in sight and sound we apprehend the supernatural and our own hearts are tossed helpless from one extreme of emotion to another.

A stranger already to the tongue of man, the immortal voice of the dead stoops once more to speak. After the first terrible greeting, when the ghostly figure rejects the earthly food proffered, how eerie, how horrifying the effect, of the irregular intervals with which his voice moves up and down the scale, as on a ladder woven of air. He demands an immediate resolve: Repent! The soul has little time left for decision and long, eternally long, is the road. Don Giovanni in his monstrous obstinacy defying the eternal laws; struggling, resisting, writhing helpless under the ever-increasing powers of Hell and at last, his gestures never losing their perfect dignity, going to his doom; whose heart and reins do not tremble with horror and fascination at the sight? It is a feeling akin to that with which one admires the magnificent spectacle of Nature's power unleashed or a splendid ship ablaze. In spite of ourselves we, as it were, side with that blind power, join in the tragedy of the inexorable course of its self-destruction.

The composer had finished. For a time nobody dared to break the silence.

"Tell us," the Countess said at last, with bated

breath, "Give us, please, an idea of what you felt that night when you put down your pen."

He turned to her with shining eyes, as if aroused from a secret reverie. He thought for a moment and then said, addressing himself both to her and to his wife.

"Well, my head was in a whirl. Sitting by the open window, I had written away at this desperate *dibattimento*, down to the chorus of the spirits, in one burning flow of inspiration. After a short rest I got up from my chair, meaning to go into your room and talk to you for a little until my blood had cooled. A sudden thought crossed my mind, making me stop short in the middle of the room." He gazed at the floor for a moment and in what followed his voice betrayed an almost imperceptible tremor of emotion. "I said to myself : 'Supposing you were to die this very night and leave your score at this point, would you have peace in your grave?' 'My eyes rested on the wick of the candle in my hand and the mountains of wax which had trickled down its side. The idea sent a swift pang through my heart. Supposing, I thought to myself, sooner or later someone else, perhaps one of those rascally Italians, were entrusted with the completion of the opera. He finds that from the Introduction to the seventeenth number, with the exception of a single piece, everything is neatly put together— ripe, healthy fruit fallen from the tree and waiting in the grass to be picked up. Only in the middle of the finale he is checked for a moment, but soon discovers that the obstacle has already been largely removed— there's a chance for him ! What a temptation to rob me of my achievement! But he would be sure to burn his fingers nicely if he tried for, after all, there's always a little band of good friends who would recognize my stamp and see that the credit went where it belonged. On this I left the room, thanking God from the bottom of my heart, but thanking your guardian angel, too, my dear little wife, for having held both his hands tenderly over your brow for such a long time, keeping you asleep like a dormouse, so that you did not call out to me once. When at last I joined you and you asked me what time it was, I brazenly swore a few hours off your age—it was actually nearly four o'clock. And now you'll understand why you couldn't get me out of bed at six in the morning and the coachman had to be sent away and ordered for the next day."

"Naturally," answered Constance, "but my clever gentleman shouldn't imagine I was so stupid as to notice nothing. You need not have made such a secret to me of your splendid spurt forward."

"That wasn't why I did it."

"I know," she said, "you didn't want to have your treasure talked about yet."

"'Hans, off with the horses' harness!' is always a painful order," cried the kindly host, "but as for me, I'm only too glad that to-morrow morning we shall not be forced to hurt the feelings of a noble Viennese coachman if Monsieur Mozart finds he cannot get out of bed."

To this indirect request to prolong their stay, in which the others warmly joined, the travellers replied by giving the pressing reasons why they must hurry on. A happy compromise was reached, however—that they would not set off too early and that the whole party should enjoy a comfortable breakfast together first.

The party had now broken up into groups, standing about and chatting. Mozart seemed to be looking for someone—the bride, apparently—but as she did not happen to be there at the moment, he naïvely put the question meant for her to Francesca, who was standing close by.

"Now, what do you think on the whole of our *Don Giovanni*? What glorious future can you see for it?"

"I shall," she said laughing, "answer this question as well as I can in the place of my cousin. It's my humble opinion that if *Don Giovanni* doesn't turn the head of the whole world, God had better shut up his music shop for a bit and give men to understand——"

"And hand men the bagpipes," cut in the uncle, "and so harden their hearts that they worship Baal."

"Heaven forbid!" laughed Mozart, "Though no doubt in the course of the next sixty or seventy years, long after I've gone, many false prophets will arise."

Eugenie now joined them with the Baron and Max and the conversation unexpectedly started up again, once more becoming serious and important; so that before the party finally broke up the composer had been greatly encouraged by more than one graceful and discerning compliment.

Not till long after midnight did the party break up; till then none of them had noticed how tired they were. Next morning (the weather was as glorious as the day before) at ten o'clock a handsome coach could be seen in the courtyard packed with the luggage of

89

the two Viennese guests. The Count, looking on with Mozart while the horses were led out of the stable, asked the composer how he liked it.

"Very much. It looks extremely comfortable."

"Well, then, give me the pleasure of keeping it as a souvenir."

"What, do you really mean it?"

"But of course!"

"Holy Sixtus and Calixtus! Constance," he called up to the window where his wife stood with the others looking out, "The carriage is to be mine. From now on you'll travel in your own coach."

He embraced the smiling donor, inspected his new property from every angle and, opening the door, jumped inside.

"I feel as rich and noble as Fortunatus!" he cried, "How their eyes will pop out in Vienna!"

"I hope," said the Countess, "to see your carriage again, wreathed in flowers, on your return from Prague."

After this gay farewell, the much praised carriage, with the departing couple, really got away, moving at a quick trot towards the highway. The Count was allowing his horses to go as far as Wittengau, where post horses were to be hired.

When fine, outstanding people have, for a short while, enlivened our home with their presence, quickening our spirits with the refreshing breath of their own and enabling us to enjoy to the utmost the pleasure of extending hospitality, their departure invariably leaves an uneasy blank—at least for the rest of the day, supposing, that is, that we are entirely thrown back upon our own resources once more.

This latter at least did not apply to the party at the castle. Francesca's parents and the elderly aunt left very shortly after. The girl herself, the bridegroom and, of course, Max, stayed on. Eugenie, with whom we are more particularly concerned here because the priceless experience had affected her more deeply than anyone else—for her, one would imagine, nothing could be amiss, dimmed or incomplete. Her perfect happiness with the man she truly loved, which had just received its formal confirmation, must surely outweigh everything else—or rather, those noble and beautiful emotions which the music had aroused in her heart must of necessity have merged with her overflowing bliss. Or it would have been so had she been able to live, that day and the day before, in the present only and could now enjoy its unclouded memory. Yet already in the evening, as Madame Mozart told her stories, she had been inwardly seized by a slight foreboding for the man whose charming presence gave her such delight; this foreboding persisted at the back of her mind during the whole of Mozart's recital, behind all the incredible fascination and the music's mystery and awe; finally she was startled and shaken by how he had casually talked about himself in the same vein. She had a conviction, an absolute conviction, that this man would rapidly and inexorably be consumed in his own flame, that his presence on earth was fleeting and ephemeral because this world was, in truth, not capable of enduring the overwhelming riches which he would lavish upon it. This and many other things weighed on her heart after she had gone to bed that evening, while the echoes of *Don Giovanni* continued to ring confusedly in her head. Only towards daybreak, exhausted, she fell asleep.

The three ladies had now settled down in the garden with their needlework and the men were keeping them company. Since the conversation naturally turned exclusively on Mozart, Eugenie made no secret of her fears. No one was inclined to share them, though the Baron knew exactly what she meant. When we ourselves are happy and in harmonious and grateful mood, we are quick to reject with all our strength any thoughts of misfortune which do not immediately concern us. And so the most telling and cheerful counter-arguments were put forward, especially by the uncle, and how readily Eugenie listened to them. A little more, and she would really have been convinced that she had seen things in too gloomy a light.

A little later, as she passed through the large drawing room upstairs, which had just been cleaned and tidied up and whose curtains of green damask, now drawn across the windows, only allowed a soft twilight to penetrate, she stopped sadly before the piano. She felt as if she were dreaming, when she thought who had been sitting there, only a few hours ago. Long and pensively she gazed at the keyboard which he had so recently touched. Then softly she shut the lid and turned the lock, putting the key in her pocket, with jealous care that no other hand should open it for a long time to come. As she left, she casually put away a few song books; a tattered page fell out of one of them—a copy of an old Bohemian

92

folksong which Francesca, and very likely she also, had sometimes sung in days gone by. She looked at it and was smitten afresh. In a mood like hers, even the most harmless coincidence easily becomes significant. Whichever way she tried to understand it, the message was such that on re-reading those simple verses, the bitter tears began to fall.

> Green grows a little fir tree,
> I know not where in the forest.
> A rosebush in a garden—
> Who can tell where?
> Think, O my soul,
> Maybe they have been chosen,
> To take root on your grave
> And to grow there.
>
> Two little black horses,
> From their grassy meadow,
> Prancing and capering,
> Trot gaily back to town.
> They will pace slowly
> When they draw your coffin.
> Perhaps—who knows?—even
> Before on those hooves,
> Loose are the shoes,
> Which now I see sparkling.